Indiscretion

SANL

INDISCRETIONS OF A MARRIED MAN

Sandra Glover

Indiscretions of a Married Man

Dedications & Acknowledgements

I would first like to give acknowledgement and thanks to my heavenly father God. For I know that without him this would not and could not be possible. He has blessed me with the talent to write and tell stories and for that I am thankful.

Although my mother is no longer here, I want to thank her for believing in me when I didn't believe in myself….. I have done it MOM and I dedicate this book, my first to you!!!!!

To the love of my life Otis- I would like to say, I love you and thank you for sharing me with the computer. My sons, Dival and Darius; I thank for their overwhelming support and for being the best sons a mother could have. To my daughter in law Latoya, my number one fan, I want to say thank you!

My sister Norma, who has watched this book go from scribble on paper to this…. I say thank you! She has encouraged me in every step of the way, pushing me when I needed to be pushed.

Indiscretions of a Married Man

She has read this book more times than me. To the rest of my siblings, I say anything is possible! Be all you can be while you can be!

Special thanks to my friends and co-workers that supported me …and to Shena I would like to say thank you, thank you, thank you for being my loudest cheerleader!

Indiscretions of a Married Man

Indiscretions of a Married Man

A novel by SONDRA GLOVER

PROLOGUE

When my wife and I took our vows three years ago, I truly believed that nothing or anyone could ever make me disregard them. Three years ago, I met a woman that I fell deeply in love with and decided that she was who I wanted to spend the rest of my life with. We vowed to love and honor each other for better or worse, not really considering the *"for worse"* part.

Sometimes in life, you are thrown a curve ball that you never see coming and all that you believe in is challenged. Well that is the situation I found myself in. I was a strong believer in the fact that there is no recovery after cheating. That is, until I was the one committing the act. Because it was me, I wanted our vows to stand. I wanted my wife to be more forgiving than I would have been if the situation was reversed and she was the one doing the cheating.

Our vows were for life and there were no exceptions, as I now realize. I often wonder if the situation were reversed would I have handled it different from my wife. Would I forgive? How much does one withstand before tossing marriage vows in the wind?

Indiscretions of a Married Man

Can we really say for better or worse and stand by it? I'm not so sure after my story…….I'll let you be the judge.

Chapter 1

As Mitchell reclined in his black leather chair with his feet comfortably set on his oak desk, enjoying what little view his office offered of Midtown, a voice came across the intercom, "Mr. Reid, your wife is on line one."

"Thank you." Andrea rarely called his office, so this was indeed a pleasant surprise. "Hey baby, what's going on?" Mitchell asked with anticipation.

"Not much, just wanted to remind you that this is the weekend Dee, Sharon and I are heading out for Biloxi. We'll probably leave shortly after work."

Andrea did not get through the first sentence before Mitchell's blood pressure quickly began to rise, "We never confirmed that you were actually going to go."

"Correction Mitchell, you never confirmed. I told you about this trip two weeks ago to give you time to get used to the idea, it is this weekend and I am going." Andrea knew there would be drama when the weekend actually came. She was prepared to stand her ground and follow through with her plans regardless of how upset Mitchell became. He had gotten pretty good with the tantrums and

Indiscretions of a Married Man

normally it worked, but not this time. Andrea had been looking forward to this weekend for three weeks. It had taken her a week to mention it to him and now that the weekend was here, she was going whether he liked it or not.

Mitchell was so upset because deep down inside he knew Andrea was going this time regardless of what he said or what attitude he threw at her. "Oh just like that, you're going? I guess it doesn't matter how the hell I feel about your little weekend does it?" He muffled his anger, trying to remain calm and not be heard in his office.

"Don't start this shit Mitchell, you knew in advance about this trip. My goodness it's only one weekend…GET OVER IT!"

"Yeah, that's right it is only one weekend but you are married, you don't get to spend one weekend away from your husband!"

"Well don't feel so left out, no one's husband is going." Andrea laughed sarcastically.

"Hell, they don't even have husbands!" Mitchell said as he noted the sarcasm in her answer. Realizing this was no help in changing her mind, he tried to reason with her, "Damn baby we don't have time together as it is with our work schedules, this is the one weekend we are both off, why can't we do something together?"

Andrea just stared into the phone and thought, "Yeah and have another boring, do nothing weekend, when hell freezes over!"

Indiscretions of a Married Man

Once Mitchell received no reply he converted back to anger, "Do you even give a damn about this marriage anymore? Because lately it sure seems that you don't!" Andrea knew it would get to this point as it always did and her only thought was getting him off the phone and to begin her weekend without his demanding ass.

"Answer me Andrea, do you give a damn or not?" Mitchell tightly asked as he tried to control his anger.

Andrea knew if she did not end this call, he would go on all day with this bullshit. After hearing quite enough she calmly said, "Mitchell, I have to go. I did not call to argue with you. I will talk with you later."

Before he could respond she disconnected the phone. He stared at the dead phone in his hand not believing his wife just hung the phone up in his face. He tried to calm his voice, as he asked his secretary to get his wife back on the phone. She dialed the number and Mitchell waited to be notified that his wife was back on the phone. "I can't believe Andrea is really going to Biloxi with Dee and Sharon, who are always looking for their next screw!" He said to himself. As Mitchell sat straight up in his recliner with hands bracing the phone, his thoughts were interrupted by his secretary's voice, "It's ringing Mr. Reid."

"Thank you." Mitchell said as he thought of what he was going to say to make her change her mind. *Ring. Ring. Ring.* It's taking her so long to answer the phone he thought as it continued to ring. *"Hi you have reached Andrea Reid, sorry I can't take your*

Indiscretions of a Married Man

call right now but if you leave your name and number I will get back to you as soon as time allows."

"She's not answering the damn phone. No problem...Okay cool. I guess it is really time for a few changes in this marriage," Mitchell thought aloud. As he hung up the phone he continued to think about his marriage. *He and Andrea had met in the checkout line at the Publix grocery store. She was checking out when he walked up to the line. Andrea was 5'7 and weighed 165 pounds. She was thick and fine. She had on a well-fitted pair of Gap jeans with a baby blue knitted halter-top. Her skin was dark chocolate and flawless; she had jet-black thick hair that was above shoulder length, which she wore straight back away from her face. It was her big sexy hazel eyes that made him fall in love with her. After 18 months of intense dating, they married in December. They had a very small and personal wedding with only family and close friends. They honeymooned on a Carnival Caribbean cruise to Bahamas for six days. Once they returned from their honeymoon Andrea moved from her parent's home into Mitchell's apartment. In her father's eyes that was his first strike.*

Their marriage was great. Mitchell couldn't believe how good his marriage was after all the horror stories he'd heard from his friends who had done it. They remained in Mitchell's apartment for six months before deciding to purchase their first home in an upscale suburb in Georgia. The subdivision was Water's Edge located in Stone Mountain. Stone Mountain was a predominately

Indiscretions of a Married Man

African American middle class neighborhood. Water's Edge subdivision was tucked deep in Stone Mountain. Andrea loved their house because it was very contemporary. Upon entering the house, the cream carpet that seemed to go on forever was what caught your attention. To the right was the formal dining room; to the left was the sunken den; behind the dining room was the eat-in kitchen and at the back of the house was the formal living room with glass across the back of the house. All four of the bedrooms were upstairs with a sitting room that overlooked the downstairs. The house offered so much comfort to them that their social life practically ceased. They worked, came home and enjoyed each other's company in their new home. That seemed to be enough for them at the time.

A year passed before it seemed that Andrea was becoming restless. They had settled into the house and she wanted to resume their social life. Mitchell had become so comfortable that he saw no reason to change anything. Andrea asked Mitchell on several occasions about the two of them going out, he was not interested, he was happy with the way things were. Andrea began going out with coworkers for a couple of hours after work. She'd just tell Mitchell she was working late. This went well for a while but then Andrea found herself wanting to do more than happy hours after work. Andrea knew what Atlanta had to offer and she wanted them to be a part of it but Mitchell was so dead set against it. The few times he agreed to go out she felt as though she were out with a bodyguard, so that was short lived. She attempted going out alone a few times but each time Mitchell showed out so bad when she'd return home that she finally just resorted to staying home to keep his mouth shut. Andrea had become so resentful of Mitchell that their sex life slowed to almost a halt and they rarely had conversations of any substance. Andrea thought if she had to be at home to keep the peace she would not sit up under him as well, therefore they spent no time together at all. They'd been married for three years and the resentment still lingered because not much had changed.

Mitchell continued to think, "I love my wife. She is still as beautiful as she was the day I met her. I am trying to be a devoted husband and stay out of temptations way, but it doesn't seem to matter to her."

"This is bullshit!" Mitchell yelled out in a jealous frustration, not caring at this point who heard him. He tried once again to call her against his better judgment. *"Hi, you have reached Andrea..."* He slammed the phone on the receiver refusing to believe his wife was not answering the phone, knowing it was him that was calling. "Damn this shit!"

Chapter 2

Indiscretions of a Married Man

Unlocking the doors to her 2015 Infiniti, Andrea asked herself the question, "Why did I even call Mitchell!" She knew before she made the call he was going to flip like he always did. This time he would have to get over it because she was going to Biloxi. Mitchell had become so comfortable with going to work, coming home and having Andrea there waiting, which had become very old to her. It would be nice to get away, if only for a weekend. They didn't go out together anymore and the few times they did Mitchell was like a damn watchdog waiting to attack. Andrea was not really sure what was going on in her husband's mind lately but he had become very jealous and it had become unbearable.

As she started her car, she thought she should go home while Mitchell was still at work to pick up her packed bags. She'd packed yesterday hoping to avoid some of his drama. She had planned this trip with her girlfriends well aware that it would be an issue at home. Mitchell was not too fond of her girlfriends.

She met them at work five years ago. Sharon, Dee, and Andrea attended a job fair that the Department of Labor was sponsoring and they were hired as IT techs with a new technology company called VTEX. They went through six weeks of training together, becoming the best of friends. They were always planning to get together outside of the job, but something would always come up…most of the time that something was Mitchell. This time they were determined not to let anything interfere with their trip to Biloxi, not even Andrea's husband.

Indiscretions of a Married Man

Mitchell was right about one thing, neither of them had a man at this time. Sharon is 32 years old and drop dead gorgeous. She is 5'7 and weighs 145 pounds; brown eyes with dark brown hair that she wears in a short bob. Sharon could turn heads on her worse day. Previously married with a seven-year-old daughter, she has sworn off any possibility of future marriage. After walking in on her husband and a 21 year old in a very compromising situation, she divorced him and refused to forgive. Her motto was, "*once a cheat always a cheat.*" Andrea thought Sharon was a little harsh, but we all have our own crosses to bear. "She's cool though, that's my girl!" Andrea said aloud. She then smiled at the thought of Dee who was totally different from Sharon.

Dee is 36 years old; she has no children and has never been married. She thought she was the last of the players and half the damn time she was the one getting played. Do not attempt to tell her she is not handling her business. She's giving up more free ass than the law allows. I believe she is trying to screw her way into wealth but it doesn't seem to be working. Dee is 4'9 and weighs in wet at 105. She's not just little, she's little and packing, she's got the curves. She pulls in plenty of eligible bachelors but she can't seem to hold them. Her hair is faded in a boy cut and it is colored blonde *of course...* but it compliments her golden complexion. She thinks she is *player of the year*. And then there's me, the married one, the hopelessly devoted wife with the overbearing husband. The three of us get along so well, although we are totally different. They tease

Indiscretions of a Married Man

me about Mitchell, but I can take it because he is my husband and regardless of his irritating demand of me being under him 24/7, I do truly love him.

As Andrea got close to home she realized she needed to go by her mom and dad's to pick up her dress from her younger sister Monica, hoping she was home.

Her phone rang as she pulled into her parent's driveway. "Sometimes I really hate this damn cell phone, but thank God for caller ID," she said as she realized the caller was Mitchell…again. Andrea turned the ignition off and Monica came out of the front door and met her sister before she opened the car door to get out. Monica took a seat on the porch.

"I'm surprised you're home." Andrea said from her car.

"Why is that?" Monica said hoping there would be no lecture.

"Well you know you're never here girl." Andrea thought their parents gave Monica entirely too much freedom to be sixteen. They were very strict when Andrea was growing up but Monica had very little supervision. Monica was Andrea's younger sister. They were years apart. Their parents had given birth to Monica when Andrea was fourteen years old. With so many years in between they never really bonded as sisters do. Andrea watched her parents raise Monica with a very relaxed hand. Initially Monica looked up to her older sister and Andrea tried to be a big sister to Monica and help her parents in raising her because of their age.

Indiscretions of a Married Man

As Monica got older and began to physically mature she became very manipulative. She was very aware of her body along with her beauty. She was 5'9 and weighed 130, flawless pecan skin, brown hair that she wore in a short natural curly style; she looked like a younger version of Andrea. She was never where she was supposed to be. She was one of those teenagers that thought they knew everything and you couldn't tell her anything. She was going to have to catch a lot of bruises from falling before she learned because she was not listening to anyone. Andrea tried to talk to Monica but she always became very irritated so to avoid confrontation with her sister she said nothing at all unless it was really necessary. While Andrea did not live in their parent's house, she made sure they were as aware of Monica's every move as she was. Monica began to despise Andrea rather than look up to her.

After Andrea married and moved in with Mitchell, Monica was overjoyed because she felt as though the warden had moved out. Monica had gotten into so much trouble with their parents because of Andrea. Therefore they were never able to establish a sister-to-sister relationship and Monica harbored nothing but feelings of envy for her sister over a period of time. Once Andrea moved out of the house she washed her hands of trying to help in disciplining Monica and chose to leave it to their parents, saying nothing at all. They got along better this way. Andrea stepped out of her car, "Monica I need my dress."

"Which dress are you talking about?"

Indiscretions of a Married Man

"My black dress with the back out, I want to take it with me to Biloxi."

"Whoa, since when are you going to Biloxi?" Monica faked surprise.

"I am leaving today with Sharon and Dee."

"That explains why I wasn't invited," Monica sighed.

"You weren't invited because you are 16 and we are 30 and over, thank you."

"Really…? What does that have to do with it?"

"It has everything to do with it little girl!" Andrea said becoming a little irritated with her sister's attitude, always thinking she was grown as her.

"Wow you're going to Biloxi and Mitchell is okay with it?" Monica asked with amusement because everyone knew how possessive Mitchell was. Andrea walked around giving advice as if she was in charge, but Monica knew that her sister couldn't use the bathroom without Mitchell wanting to wipe her ass. "Yes Mitchell knows and yes he's okay with it." Andrea lied.

"Please, give me a damn break! Oh my bad...." Monica said.

"Yeah he probably knows but I bet he is not happy about it. Are you saying he approves?" Monica knew her sister was standing there telling a big lie.

"Please Monica, I think approve is the wrong word. He's fine with it!" Andrea said not wanting to feed in to what Monica was trying to say.

Indiscretions of a Married Man

"Since you'll be in Biloxi, can I stay at your place and check out some cable?"

"Mom and dad haven't got cable yet? What's the problem?" Andrea knew any chance Monica could get away from home she would.

"You know mom and dad, Mr. and Mrs. Budget. They have basic cable. Heck I want to watch some real TV shows. I can't even check out Love and Hip Hop, you know?"

"Monica I really don't mind you going over to watch TV while Mitchell is at work, but call him to find out what time he will be home so that you can be gone before he comes home. He doesn't like anybody in the house when we're not home and that includes you. Make sure it's okay with him before you go over to the house and don't be surprised if he says no because I'm thinking he might not be in the best of moods this evening." Andrea already knew that Mitchell was not going to allow Monica to come over to watch television; he cherished his privacy too much. Rather than tell her sister no, she would leave that up to Mitchell, he had gotten so good at it.

"Sure I'll make sure I call before I go over there." Monica said although she had no intention of asking Mitchell just so he could say no, when all she wanted to do was catch up on Love and Hip Hop.

"Now give me my dress so I can be on my way. Do you still have the spare key to my place?" Andrea asked.

17

Indiscretions of a Married Man

"Yeah," Monica said as she went into her closet and pulled Andrea's black dress out. She didn't want to give the dress back. It was a nice and sexy dress. "Here's your dress but I want it back."

"Don't hold your breath and please make sure you call Mitchell before you go there." Andrea said again knowing her sister tended to do what she wanted regardless of what she was told. "Oh before I get out of here let me have my house key."

"Damn, I have to go look for it; it's in my room somewhere. You got time to wait?" Monica asked.

No I really don't. Dee and Sharon are waiting on me. I will get my key when I get back." Andrea said as she opened the door to get back into her car. As she pulled off she wondered just what her sister was up to. Monica probably planned on being somewhere other than Andrea's house, she has never been that interested in cable, especially on a Friday night, Andrea thought. Whatever Monica's plans were, Andrea knew Mitchell was no pushover and he wouldn't go for it.

Chapter 3

As Mitchell got into his Nissan Maxima, he enjoyed the good feeling of going home after a long day of work, some of his hardest work had come from pissed off motivation. "I guess I can thank Andrea for such a productive day." He laughed at the thought. He pulled out of the parking lot and drove towards home. He assumed that because he had not heard from his wife since this afternoon, that

Indiscretions of a Married Man

she decided to go on her little outing, regardless of his feelings on the matter. "Well, I am not going to worry myself over it tonight," he said aloud.

As he pulled into their driveway, it brought on a lonely feeling, realizing just how big their house was and knowing Andrea wasn't in there. "Hell, maybe she's inside waiting for me," nice thought but not likely Mitchell told himself. As he sat in the car for a minute waiting for the garage door to begin to rise, he realized they had issues that would have to be dealt with when Andrea returned from Biloxi.

Mitchell pulled into the garage looking towards their bedroom window because it looked as though a dim light were on in it. The master bedroom was located on the front side of the house right over the garage. Maybe Andrea didn't go after all, Mitchell thought as he put his key into the lock. He felt his excitement slowly rising with the thought of Andrea being upstairs, thinking he had gotten his way again. Once inside the house he realized how nice and quiet it was. He closed the front door and looked up the stairs where the glimmer of light was coming from. He just smiled with excitement. His excitement hit the top, now convinced that his wife was upstairs waiting for him. He thought to himself, "I am going to give her just what she is up there waiting for. Deciding he didn't want to waste time taking his clothes off once upstairs, he wanted to surprise her as well so he began taking them off right at the front door. He removed his clothes so quickly that by the time he reached

Indiscretions of a Married Man

the bedroom door he was naked. When he walked through the bedroom door in his naked form he wanted his wife to know exactly what he expected and maybe she wouldn't be able to deny him or herself this time. Mitchell whispered as he stepped through the bedroom door naked, "Baby, I am so glad you decided not to go. I'm sorry about today. All the way home tonight I've been hoping that you didn't go. Thank you"

She slowly lifted her head from under the blanket and called his name very softly, "Mitchell"...

"Yes baby it's me," Mitchell answered in barely a whisper, too excited with the thought of what a good make up session this was going to be. Smiling to herself as she peeped from under the blanket she said, "My bad Mitchell, it's me. Andrea left this afternoon. What are you doing here? I thought that you and Andrea were gone for the weekend. I didn't think y'all would mind so I crashed for the night." While speaking her practiced lie, Monica could not take her eyes off of Mitchell's body, as he stood in the doorway naked. Mitchell stood 6'3 and looked as though he weighed in at 210 pounds. His entire body looked as though it had been chiseled, muscles right where they belonged. His skin was the color of midnight. He had perfect white teeth and his hair was cut even and very low. "Damn, brother-in-law is fine as hell!" She thought to herself but said aloud, "I see the gym is paying off."

If ever there were a true moment of embarrassment, this was it. Monica was having no problem whatsoever staring him down like he was a T-bone and that is exactly what he felt like. Trying his best to be cool and at the same time grabbing for something to cover his naked ass up, he managed to grab a pair of boxer underwear out of his chest drawer since all of his clothes were at the bottom of the steps. "Monica, what the hell are you doing here?" Mitchell said through clenched teeth.

"Andrea said ya'll were going out of town and no one would be here tonight."

"Well I am home and I would appreciate it if you got your ass out of my damn bed! Even if we were not home what gives you the damn right to make yourself at home in our shit!" Mitchell said as he turned the wall light switch on. "Get your ass out of my bed!" As much as he hated to say it he felt himself getting slightly, no, very much aroused by the fact that she was watching him so intensely. As Mitchell pulled on his underwear he thought, "Why would Andrea let her sister spend the night while she is out of town? I don't believe this girl is telling the truth. She's been known to lie and she needs to hurry up and get out of my bed! As horny as I am I don't need this shit!" Mitchell expected to get in bed with his wife and instead comes home to her under aged sister. He needed to get her out of here now before his judgment became clouded.

"I didn't think you'd be here. Andrea said you two were going to Biloxi. I'll get up out of your bed. Sorry it's just I didn't think you'd be here so it wouldn't be a problem." Monica said.

Indiscretions of a Married Man

"Well you thought wrong and I am here so get your ass out of my bed…now!" Mitchell slightly yelled getting a little frustrated.

"Do you mind if I stay in one of the other rooms, it's too late for me to call for a ride unless you want to take me?" Monica said with no intentions of leaving at all. She had plans for her sister's husband, just as she had planned this. Everything was going according to her plan.

"Sleep in any room you want to, that is where you should have been if you were going to be here. Why the hell would you plop your ass in our bed? I am too tired to take you home tonight but you need to be gone in the morning, thank you." Mitchell responded, watching as she sat up in the bed and begin to pull the comforter and sheet back to get out of the bed. She had a very sexy and conniving smile on her face and he began to wonder what the hell was there to smile about. She was taking her sweet time about getting up so Mitchell thought he would rush her a bit because this situation was becoming too intense for him. "Come on speed it up Monica!" he yelled.

"I'm getting up, you don't have to yell!" she said.

"Yeah but not quick enough, now get a move on it!" He said as he turned his back toward her. He didn't want to stare at her the way she had stared at him so he redirected his stare in a different direction. It was getting a little uncomfortable in the room. She still had that little smirk on her face; she seemed to really be enjoying the moment, well not at his expense. Mitchell turned to face her,

Indiscretions of a Married Man

prepared to scream on her again. He prepared to stare at her with the intention of making her uncomfortable but was not prepared for what he saw. Monica completely pulled the cover back and stepped out of the bed with nothing on but a thong panty. She was damn near naked. His throat got so tight he could hardly breathe. He didn't know what to do. He couldn't say a word nor could he peel his eyes from her fine body. His mind kept screaming, "Oh man, she is so fine." She slowly got out of the bed; very aware of the effect she was having on him. Still smiling Monica tried to get by Mitchell, purposely brushing up against him. Mitchell didn't try to move. He didn't want to move. Monica looked at him the entire time. Mitchell asked, "Where in the hell are your ugh, clothes? "

"I'm getting them, they're in the bathroom." Monica lied.

Mitchell thought to himself, "why is she just standing here, she's standing so close to me that I can smell her, I can smell her breath, and even her body odor. Before his brain could register the word "leave" Monica had her lips on his, something she had wanted to do for a very long time. Mitchell did not try to fight her, he couldn't. It had been a couple of weeks since he had sex and twice as long with someone who was as excited about it as he was. It was then that Mitchell realized he wanted her just like she wanted him. He was caught up in the moment and blinded by who this was or what it was. He wrapped his arms around her nakedness forcing her lips apart with his tongue. Her kiss was so tender and her mouth so welcoming. She felt so soft. He couldn't keep his hands off of her.

Indiscretions of a Married Man

She eased back toward the bed and Mitchell followed, never once removing his hands or mouth from her body. Once on the bed it seemed like they were lost in each other. Monica practically ripped off his boxers like she had seen it done in the movies. This was something Andrea did not do and Mitchell was turned up all the way. He thought for her to be so young, she was aggressive. She rolled on top and straddled him. He was so excited that he couldn't take the foreplay. He reached down to put his erect penis between her swollen lips where she was sloppy wet. He began to push and realized that she was a virgin! As hot as she carried herself, who would have thought Ms. Monica was a virgin. Slowly he began to work his penis into her. She moaned in pain and for a moment tightened up and then she slowly she began to move with him. Instead of moaning in pain she was now moaning how good it felt to her. "Mitchell, you feel so good." Monica moaned. Mitchell was lost in the feeling of the moment. He couldn't believe what he was hearing. It was a nice sound and it felt so good that he couldn't stop. He wasn't sure if it was because it was a new feeling or because he was horny as hell. The one thing he was sure about was that this was not right but it felt too good and he was in too deep to worry about it now. Monica rocked herself back and forth on top of Mitchell, making him feel too damn good to think about the reality of it. He had to keep telling himself to slow down. Hold on to this feeling for as long as you can. Mitchell pulled her off of him and laid her on her stomach. He slid down the length of her body until he was

Indiscretions of a Married Man

between her legs. He stared down at her apple shaped ass and knew he had to go there. Knowing that she was so young he was sure this would be too much for her so he thought he would need to prime her into readiness. Mitchell placed a hand on each of her ass cheeks and spread them. He slid his tongue up and down the middle of her ass. She moaned and that just made him more excited. He began to penetrate her ass with his tongue. She began to squirm and the more she squirmed the deeper he plunged his tongue into her. She was so caught up in the feeling that she didn't realize Mitchell had substituted his tongue with his finger. He had wet her ass up so much that his finger just slid right in. He slid his finger in and out, until he loosened her ass up. He slid his finger out and slid his body up over hers. Monica didn't realize what Mitchell's next move was. She was so hot that she arched her back and tooted her ass up in the air, thinking he was going to penetrate her vagina from the back. Mitchell thought to himself, "Damn she is a little freak!" He parted her ass cheeks and began to glide his penis into her anus. Once Monica felt a quick jab, her entire body tightened up. She thought he had made a mistake and slipped into the wrong hole but as Mitchell continued to push forward, she realized he was where he wanted to be. She tried to protest and wiggle him out but he had her in a compromising position and she could not escape his penetration. She felt a sharp pain as Mitchell thrust a final time, putting himself deep inside of her ass. She broke into a sweat and her body fell weak. Mitchell was oblivious to any of her protest and he continued

Indiscretions of a Married Man

to grind into her ass. Once he was as deep as he could get, he began to slow stroke in and out. After her initial shock of the pain, Monica laid still for a moment to recover from the pain. Then she began to slowly throw her ass back at him. Mitchell grabbed her by her waist practically lifting her off of the bed as he exploded into her ass. Exhausted he rolled off of her to cool off. Within minutes he was passed out. Monica lay with a smile on her face, thinking how spectacular their session was. She couldn't sleep because although Mitchell came, she had not.

    As she watched him sleep she began to rub between her legs. She crawled on top of Mitchell and began to grind but he would not get stiff enough for her to ride. She got off of him and took him in her mouth. She had never done oral sex before but had seen it done enough in the movies. Mitchell began to moan, as he became alert and realized what was going on; he reached down and grabbed the back of Monica's head, ramming himself down her throat. She gagged several times but because he had a hold of the back of her head, she could not escape him thrusting deep in her throat. He came close to coming but didn't want to do that in her mouth, so he pulled out and pushed her on her back. He lifted her legs over his shoulders and slid his penis back into her ass. She was sloppy wet and this time it felt good to her. She began throwing herself back at him and he thrust harder and harder. She came for the first time in her life and thought, "Oh my goodness! This is the best feeling in

Indiscretions of a Married Man

the world!" Once Mitchell realized she was coming he joined her and afterwards they both passed out.

The rest of the weekend consisted of pretty much the same, never once did Andrea call and at this point it didn't seem to matter. All Mitchell focused on was that he was totally satisfied and did not want this weekend to end. He looked over at Monica and thought, "I'm going to drink this up like it's my last glass of water."

CHAPTER 4

It's Sunday morning; the sun is shining so brightly through the bedroom window that it awakens him. He realizes that the weekend is over and the good time has come to an end. Monica is still asleep, snuggled under Mitchell like he was her blanket. She was very different from Andrea. She was so needy or maybe it was that she was so young and just didn't know any better. The shit feels different and Mitchell had to admit his ego was stroked in the worse way. As much as he hated for this weekend to end, he needed to wake Monica up because Andrea would be in at six tonight and it was already 12:45. This was one weekend he would never forget. As reality began slipping in, he didn't want to admit it but he fucked up.

"I should have never let this shit happen and I damn sure should never have let it last the entire weekend. I need to be kicked in my ass because I know this girl is too young for me to have had in my

Indiscretions of a Married Man

bed. Not only is she young but she is my wife's sister," he argued with himself. What the hell did I do? My weak ass has created a situation that could have been prevented and will probably blow up in my face. I've got to make sure Monica knows that this is not a relationship. She needs to realize that this was a one-time thing that will not ever happen again. She has to be made to understand this cannot get out.

"Monica, baby wake up, it's time to crawl your sleepy ass out of bed. It is 1:00 and Andrea will be home in a couple of hours. I've got to put things back in order." Mitchell thought, "She's sexy as hell laying here. I could look at her all day but that's not about to happen today. I wish she would get up before I get up on her again." As he laid there thinking about it, Monica just rolls over and climbs aboard. He rolled her back over and took charge of this thing. It felt so good. "I could get so use to this. I wonder is it because she is a forbidden fruit that making me so crazy. How am I going to handle this when Andrea gets back? "I have really screwed up. He whispered in her ear, "Oh baby this feels so good. I can't seem to get enough of you."

"Mitchell, don't worry, it's all for you, just for you", Monica whispered back.

Now normally that would have been some real sweet shit to hear, just what it would take to put a man over the edge. But for some reason it did just the opposite to me. As a matter of a fact it snapped my ass right out of pillow talk and into reality one more

Indiscretions of a Married Man

time. He rolled off and sat up in the bed, looked down at Monica and braced myself for this little conversation they were about to have.

"Mitchell, what's wrong?" she said sounding like innocence.

"Monica, I need for you to understand that Andrea is coming home at six o'clock tonight and once she gets back we cannot do this again. This should have never happened. I know it's a little late to say it but it's true and it can't ever happen again. Do you understand what I'm saying Monica? No one, absolutely no one can ever know about this, okay?" Mitchell began to wonder where her parents thought she was this weekend and asked, "Monica where do your parents think you've been this weekend?"

"Don't worry they think I spent this weekend with Deb. I understand what you're saying. Don't worry. Why would I tell? I'm not some kid that runs her mouth you know."

"I just want to make sure we understand each other Monica. I know you're not a kid. I just don't want this to turn ugly. You know Andrea would have no understanding of this." He said hoping she truly understood.

"Stop worrying Mitchell," Monica said.

What the hell is that smile on her face for? I think she really believes this is some kind of game. She better recognize that I am not playing with her young ass. I don't want to have to break my foot… • Hell, I need to stop tripping. It's too late for that, Mitchell thought.

29

Indiscretions of a Married Man

"Okay Monica, party is over, get up so I can get this place in order."

"Guess we're not going to finish what we started, huh?"

"No baby, I want you to get dressed so I can get you out of here and get this place cleaned up."

"Okay, but this is the last taste you'll get." Monica said as she looked at Mitchell and thought, he thinks this is it, but I've got news for him. I am not done with him yet. He sure has picked the wrong time to start worrying. We have spent the entire weekend in their bed and now his ass wants to worry. Well he sure wasn't worried while we were doing it and he is good. No wonder Andrea puts up with his jealous shit. Bro-in-law has it going on and he goes non-stop. He acts like he's starved for sex or he has one hell of an appetite. Wait until I tell Deb. She is never going to believe this. All that bragging she did about being with a real man. Raymond is only 18 years old, excuse me but that is not a man. I want to see her top this shit. I just won't tell her who he is, that might not sit too tight with her. Monica began to stroke her own ego. I knew I had it! I can pull any man I want, including my stuck up sister's husband, "How do you like me now Andrea?" She talks all that bullshit like she has her shit so together. Sometimes I really hate listening to her so-called advice on life and men. Huh, she can't tell me a damn thing ever again because she can't even keep her MAN satisfied, look who did that, her sixteen year old sister that she always wants to give advice to. "Yes!" Monica said aloud as she showered.

Indiscretions of a Married Man

Chapter 5

I hope this weekend has given Mitchell enough time to cool himself down. Sometimes he just goes over the edge about little things. This trip sure was one of pleasure. Since this was our first time going to Biloxi we all had the gambler fever. We spent the entire weekend in the damn casino on the slot machine. Well at least Sharon and I did. As always, Dee was trying to get her groove on. She did get lost a couple of times but that's just Dee. Well the fun is over, time to go back to the old routine.

"Man, am I glad to see home. It looks like Mitchell is here," Andrea said to herself. "I hope he doesn't start his shit because I am really not in the mood. I am tired and would like to sleep soundly in my bed." As Andrea put her key in the lock she braced herself for the bullshit that waited for her on the other side of the door. She opened the front door quietly hoping not to disturb Mitchell. Once inside she realized how quiet it was. It's too damn quiet and I know he's not sleep it's only 8:45. Well I won't push my luck I better enjoy the quiet time. Andrea turned on the hall light so that she wouldn't trip over his mess. He probably hasn't cleaned since I left. After quietly walking through the downstairs, Andrea whispered, "I must be in the wrong house because this downstairs is spotless."

Indiscretions of a Married Man

She then smiled to herself as she vainly thought," maybe this little trip has taught him appreciation! Andrea went up the stairs and still not one trace of a mess. She walked into the bedroom and Mitchell was spread across the bed knocked out. "Good!" Andrea whispered. This makes it easier to sweep the drama under the table and make up a little since he is already in the position. Andrea showered in the guestroom not wanting to wake Mitchell until she was ready. Just the thought of what was to come excited her tremendously.

The shower felt so good and to Andrea there was no place like home, especially when you're talking shower and bed. It had been a long weekend, she thought about what went on with her and Mitchell before she left for Biloxi. Their relationship had not been so good, but she had a little time to think while in Biloxi and realized that Mitchell was going to be Mitchell no matter what. He was jealous, possessive and overbearing when she met him and that's just who he was. She loved him for who he was and it made no sense to get so mad about it now. Nothing had really changed about him. Andrea was all showered and ready for bed and Mitchell. She crawled between the fresh sheets and looked at Mitchell, "Damn my baby looks good laying here. I really want to make love to him." This surprised Andrea because it had been a long time since she felt like this. Maybe absence does do a lot for a relationship.

"Baby I'm home and I am going to show you how much I missed you." Andrea whispered as she felt the warmth from his body and it was a nice feeling since the sheets were cold. She

Indiscretions of a Married Man

snuggled under him; his body scent drifting up her nose made her warm all over. "I want you so bad," Andrea whispered in Mitchell's ear. Damn he must have had a hard weekend while I was gone because he's out cold, Andrea thought. Normally I wouldn't do this but I've got to give him what he likes sometime and tonight I think I may like it too. I had new outlook on my marriage and realized that Mitchell wasn't the only one at fault. I hadn't been keeping up my end of our relationship either. Andrea was willing to start right here with change, she had really missed him. She moved closer to him and thought he would awaken once he felt her next to him but he did not. He seemed to be very tired, which was the only time he snored. She was snuggled tightly under him and he had not budged. She kissed his neck and slowly moved her kisses to his chest. Slipping her head under the sheets she began kissing his stomach, sticking her tongue into his belly button. Mitchell began slowly arching his lower back. "Ah, we have movement, I knew it wouldn't take long," Andrea thought as she slowly ran her tongue down to his penis and took him into her mouth. Mitchell was coming to life. He slowly moved his hips.

"Andrea, I'm so glad your home. I missed you baby, damn I missed you", Mitchell moaned as Andrea took more of him into her mouth. Mitchell wanted her to keep doing what she was doing.

"Things will be better baby." Andrea said taking him out of her mouth long enough to make her promise and then returned to the oral love she was giving him.

Indiscretions of a Married Man

As Mitchell rose to the occasion he slowly removed Andrea's mouth from his penis and pulled her up over his face. He pulled her down on his face as he began to lick her. He slid his tongue inside of her, making love to her with mouth. His objective was to satisfy her. "I love you baby." Mitchell moaned as he began to lose control.

"I love you too." Andrea smiled with satisfaction.

Chapter 6

Monica pondered in thought as she stared at the phone as if trying to will it to ring. Andrea's been home a week and Mitchell hasn't called me, I wonder what's up. I sure wouldn't mind seeing him again. He was so good. But that's just a thought; I know he won't see me with Andrea back home or would he? There's only one way to find out. What's that number at his office? Monica shifted through her papers to find Mitchell's office number. As she began to dial the number, she thought this would really surprise him. The telephone rang twice before Tonya answered, "Good Afternoon, Thank you for calling GBS, how may I direct your call?"

"May I speak with Mr. Reid please?" Monica tried to disguise her voice with professionalism.

"May I ask who is calling?" asked Tonya.

"Ms. Brown."

"Please hold, while I connect."

"Mr. Reid, there is a Ms. Brown on line one for you."

"Thank you Tonya." What the hell does Monica want? I knew this was coming; it's been a whole week and not one word from her. Just when I thought it was safe to relax and forget she does a friendly reminder.

"This is Mitchell, what is it Monica?" Mitchell asked in a hurried and hostile tone.

"Hey Mitchell, just calling to check on you, haven't heard from you since Andrea got back in town."

"Did you expect to?" Mitchell said as cold as he could.

"Well yeah, I was kind of hoping you'd call."

"Look Monica, I thought we got an understanding before you left the house. Let me refresh your little memory, I am married to your sister. What happened with us should have never happened and I am sorry it did, but it cannot happen again! It's my fault that it did, I take all the blame for it but I love Andrea and you have got to understand that. Do you?"

"I guess I have no other choice. I was thinking about the weekend we spent together and thought maybe you may want to try to see each other sometime." She suddenly sounded like a small child.

"That absolutely will not happen again Monica. What we had was sex, that's it, nothing more and please do not try to make it into anything more than that! I am sorry it happened but I can tell

Indiscretions of a Married Man

you that it's not going to happen again. Am I making myself clear? I think you are a beautiful young lady. But I am too old for you and I am married to your sister. You deserve more." Mitchell hated to be so harsh with her but he had to make her understand their wrong.

"Yes, I hear you loud and clear Mitchell. It was only a thought. Don't worry I won't bother you again."

The phone went dead in Mitchell's hand before he could say good-bye. "I truly hope she does understand." He was beginning to get nervous about this mess and he was starting to believe that it was not going to disappear as quietly as he hoped.

After Monica hung the phone up, her mouth hung open in disbelief. She thought aloud, "I cannot believe that arrogant bastard! He spends the whole weekend all up in my ass, I couldn't keep him off of me and now he wants to pull that "*I love your sister*" shit, please. I can't get over his bullshit! That's okay though, I won't blow up his spot." Monica wanted to show Mitchell he couldn't just kick her to the curb but knew she couldn't because her family would kick her ass to the curb. "He can go to hell! Let Andrea have his cheating ass!" Monica really needed someone to talk with and her best friend Debra Taylor was not back yet. Debra's father had taken the family away for the weekend. He is a real family man, Mr. Police Officer. He's a pretty nice man, kind of different from my dad. I can't remember the last time we've done anything as a family. My dad has his own agenda, as does my mom. It works for us, although there are times when I wouldn't mind being like Debra

Indiscretions of a Married Man

and her parents. She says it's lame, but when she comes back you can tell she has had a good time. "Damn I'll be glad when Debra gets back in town." Monica said aloud still thinking about Mitchell.

Chapter 7

As Mitchell left the office heading home he began to wonder what had come over Andrea since she had returned from Biloxi. She was like a totally different person. "This is the Andrea I remember marrying," he thought. She's been back over a week now and everything was great. She'd made love to him every night since she's been back. It's like we've just met. That new and exciting feeling, I find myself rushing through the day just to get to her. She came in from Biloxi last Sunday night and I was out cold recovering from my sinful weekend. Andrea climbed into bed and took charge, which was something she hadn't done in a very long time. "Damn that was one hell of a night. We made love all night with very little conversation." No reason to rehash the argument we had before she left. Since she chose not to bring it up, I did the same. No words were needed for apologies; our bodies said it all.

Later on the next morning Andrea did ask me had Monica called or come by over the weekend, something about her wanting to hang out and watch cable television. She threw me for a minute

Indiscretions of a Married Man

because according to Monica, Andrea told her we were both going to Biloxi and she took it upon herself to pop up. Now listening to Andrea, it seems that was a lie told by Monica. So she knew I would be home. That little conniving bitch! She had the whole thing planned. She banked on the fact that I wouldn't resist and she was right. Damn! Damn! Damn! I have a feeling that this is not going anywhere before it gets ugly and I was really trying to forget that shit, especially since making up was going so good with Andrea. I just replied by saying, no she never made it. I was so glad she didn't push it because I was not prepared to lie any further. I had not thought of a lie good enough. "I swear I hope that this shit doesn't blow in my face. But for some reason I think it may," Mitchell said to himself. Monica called me at the job today, for what? She can't possibly think that I am going to get with her again, especially while her sister, my damn wife is here. What the hell is wrong with her? Mitchell asked himself nervously. I basically told her she was just a piece ass for the weekend. I really hate that I had to be so blunt with her but I hope she got it this time. Mitchell's thoughts began to center on his act of infidelity. As he thought sincerely to himself, he began questioning himself, "What makes a man screw up the way he just did?" It's all good while it's going on, you block out the consequences, getting lost in the moment, and when the moment is over, the "what have I done", sets in. Finally feeling so good about his marriage and knowing that his moment of weakness could and probably would explode in his face at anytime, Mitchell dropped his head in his hands and began to cry as he whispered, *"What have I done, Lord what have I done…"*

Chapter 8

The phone rang and Monica rushed to answer, "Hello." Monica immediately recognized her best friend's voice and began to smile.

"Hello, is Monica home?" Debra asked.

"It's me girl! Don't tell me you been gone so long you can't tell my voice. Some kind of best friend you are!"

"I'm sorry girl; it's not like that, what's going on?" Debra said, happy to hear her friend's voice.

"Same thing, different day," Monica said calmly. She didn't want to sound like some excited little kid in a rush to share her story. "Debra, I've got some shit to tell you", Monica whispers, not able to hold on to her secret.

"What's up girl? Debra knew it had something to do with a guy because that was all Monica thought about.

"Who's at home with you?" Monica asked.

"No one is here but me. I'm not sure where my mom and dad are but one of the cars is still in the garage so I am assuming they're together. I'm not doing anything, come on by."

Indiscretions of a Married Man

"Okay be there in 15." Monica was so glad Debra was back. She missed her, they could talk about anything and there was never judgment passed. Debra only lived three blocks away so Monica could walk.

"Mom, I'm going to Deb's. I'll be home later." She hoped her mother wouldn't try to make her clean up before she left.

"Alright be back before dark or call."

"Yeah mom, okay." As Monica walked the three blocks she prepared her story for Debra. She knew Debra would not believe her but she did not care she just needed to tell someone. Especially after Mitchell had the nerve to dismiss her like she was a trick. As she knocked at the Taylor's front door she had to remind herself not to say his name.

Debra opened the door after the first knock, "Damn girl, did you run over here? You got here fast, what's up?"

"Go to hell Debra."

"Come on in. I was in my room trying to get a puff without smelling up the room or house."

"….puff of what girl?"

"Nothing but a Newport, you want one?" Debra asked knowing Monica didn't smoke cigarettes.

"No thanks you know me, if it isn't a blunt, I don't want." Debra burst out laughing at the way Monica expressed herself. She had a way of saying things. "You crack me up with your damn sayings."

40

Indiscretions of a Married Man

"Whatever…."

"So go ahead spill your guts. I know your dying to."

"Okay your right, I have to tell you…"

"Wait let me get my cigarette," Debra said as she lit her Newport and began to slowly inhale.

Debra was standing by the window puffing away while Monica was seated on Debra's bed trying to be her lookout while she smoked since she wasn't too concerned. Monica thought it awfully bold of Debra to be getting her smoke on with her bedroom door open like her parents were never coming home. The way her bedroom was set up you would never even know if someone was coming because you could not see around the corner until someone was right in your face, by then it would be too late.

"Okay Monica, I am ready. Talk…"

"Turn the stereo down, so I don't have to yell and we can hear when someone comes in."

"Stop being so paranoid Monica." Debra said as she barely turned the stereo volume down.

"Swear you won't say anything Deb."

"Come on now, you know better than that."

"Debra, while you were gone I spent the weekend with a man!" Monica said not able to hide her excitement.

"Quit lying Monica?"

"I am not lying. I promise you I spent the entire weekend with an older man."

Indiscretions of a Married Man

"What is older Monica? What was he 18, 19 years old?" Debra thought that Monica was exaggerating.

"Please, I know the difference, you don't. Can we say 33 years old?" Monica knew she had Debra's attention now.

"Monica, we don't even know any guys over 20." Debra said refusing to believe her.

"Maybe you don't, but I do."

"Who do you know over 20? Huh? Well who the hell is he?" Debra pushed.

"I can't tell you that. Anyway that's not important."

"Why isn't it? Do I know him?"

"Alright Perry Mason enough of the questions." Monica refused to give the name.

"Okay, okay, so what did you do and where did you stay?" Debra wanted to hear details now.

"We stayed at his house, and stayed in his bed the whole weekend!"

"What did you tell your mom and dad? Where do they think you stayed?"

"Well they don't think I stayed with him crazy."

"Hell, where did you tell them you were?

"They think that I stayed with you."

"Monica what if they check with my mom or dad, then what?" Debra hated when Monica involved her in her lies without asking her first.

Indiscretions of a Married Man

"They won't."

"Yeah, that's what you say."

"Anyway let me finish Deb. I stayed over his house the whole weekend. Girl, he is a real man not a boy. And believe me there is a difference."

"What do you mean by that? Did you hear the door?"

"No Debra, what door, I thought you said nobody was here." Monica had gotten so involved in telling her story she forgot about caution.

"Nobody's here but I thought I heard something."

"Well stop tripping."

"Okay tell me what you mean there is a difference?"

"Well Debra, he kissed me from head to toe!"

"You are lying!"

"No I am not lying. He came home and I pretended to be knocked out in his bed with nothing on. I got out of his bed and tried to walk past him. He couldn't take it. He laid my ass on that bed and started kissing me in my mouth and girl his mouths just kept going lower and lower, till his face was in the coochie."

"Quit lying Monica, you trying to tell me that this man ate your coochie?"

"Yes and that's the first time anyone has ever done that to me. He licked me from front to back and then turned me over and licked me from back to front!"

Indiscretions of a Married Man

"Are you dating him now? 33 is too old Monica no matter how good the sex." Debra could not believe her friend. This was a little too much for her to grasp.

"No, can you believe that bastard told me he doesn't want to see me again! Andrea returns from her trip and he kicks me to the damn curb!" Monica had become so upset when she thought about the conversation Mitchell and her had earlier in the week that she had not realized she mentioned her sister's name.

"Did you just say Andrea?" Debra was shocked.

"What are you crazy? Of course I didn't say Andrea's name!" Monica knew she had really screwed up because she knew Debra would not let it go until she admitted to it.

"Monica, I know what I heard and you said Andrea! You fucked your sister's husband! How could you do that Monica? Oh my god, what are you going to do when she finds out?"

"She won't find out Debra. You said you wouldn't say anything!"

"Do you dislike your sister that much? She really loves Mitchell, that's her husband, how could you? I won't say anything Monica, but that's some pretty foul shit you've done." Debra just stared at her friend not believing what she had just heard. Together they had done some things neither of them was proud of, but this was more than she was prepared to hear. Debra could do nothing but stare at Monica. She was speechless.

Indiscretions of a Married Man

"...Anyway he was the one who wanted me Deb! He came on to me!" Monica said as she tried to fix her admission.

"That is not what you said earlier. It doesn't matter you've already done it and I really don't want to talk about it anymore." Debra wanted Monica to leave but didn't have the nerve to ask her to go.

Debra and Monica were so caught up in their conversation earlier, that they never heard Debra's father come in the house nor did they notice him outside of Debra's bedroom door for the last 20 minutes.

Chapter 9

As John Taylor dialed the Brown residence he tried to prepare what he would say to Monica's parents. He was a detective but he wanted to speak to them as a friend. Not believing what he had overheard minutes ago after returning from his walk, he knew Monica's parents needed to know what he had heard. Earlier he parked his car in the garage and decided the day was too beautiful to let go to waste. He decided to take a nice long walk through the neighborhood. After walking for an hour, he returned home.

John Taylor was a quiet man and most of the time you never heard him when he entered the home. Often he would be in the house and you would never even know he was there. Well that was

Indiscretions of a Married Man

the case today. John entered the house and heard Debra's stereo playing louder than it needed to be. Because John had to pass Debra's room to get to the master bedroom, he would stop at her door and suggest she decrease the volume to the stereo. As he made his way toward Debra's room he heard another voice and recognized it was the voice of Monica Brown. She was his daughter's best friend.

The closer he came to the door the more he heard of the conversation they were having. His intent was not to eavesdrop on their conversation but the bits and pieces that he was hearing prevented him from moving away from the door. After hearing more than he wanted to, John decided to pay the Brown's a visit. John and Ben had developed a casual friendship through their daughters. They never really got together and went out due to their demanding schedules but they occasionally had a beer together. John phoned Ben before leaving out to pay him a visit.

As the garage door opened, Debra looked out of the window to see who was coming but instead she saw her dad leaving. The expression that instantly took over Debra's face told Monica that she really did hear a door open earlier. Although she didn't want to worry, Monica began to feel very uneasy at the thought that this may be the day that would change her family's life forever.

Indiscretions of a Married Man

Chapter 10

Ben Brown walked towards the door as the doorbell rung. His mind was bouncing a mile a minute, wondering what John could possibly want to talk about. He sounded like it was very urgent over the phone and Ben did not have a good feeling about this. Opening the front door Ben nervously greeted John, "Hey John what's going on man?" From past experience John knew not to beat around the bush in a situation like this one. The best approach was to be as direct and honest as possible.

"Ben I think this is something that you and Helen should hear together."

Ben began to get an uneasy feeling of worry. "Helen baby, come on in here and let's hear what John has got to tell us."

"Okay Ben, be right there," Helen said as she walked into the room.

"Hey there John, now what's this all about?" Helen said, not really worried about what John had to say to them.

"Well I am not exactly sure how you and Ben are going to handle this, but today Monica came by the house and as usual her and Debra were in the room doing their girl thing. Apparently they did not hear me come through the door because if they had they would have cut their conversation short. I walked up on Monica telling Debra that she had met an older man and that she spent the weekend with him. I am not sure which week end but I am going to

Indiscretions of a Married Man

assume it was the weekend that I took Debra and her mom out of town."

"What did she mean older, how much older?" Helen burst out before John could say another word. Then Ben remembered that was the weekend Monica said she was with Debra for the entire weekend.

"I overheard her say that you thought she was over at our place for the weekend. If I heard her correctly she said the man was 33 years old."

"Damn it! I don't know what the hell is wrong with that girl but she has just cashed in her ticket for a long overdue ass kicking. When I find out who this bastard is and I will, he is going to spend a long time looking through bars!"

"Ben, baby, try to stay calm please."

"Calm my ass Helen! Are you hearing what he has just said? Some 33 year old perverted ass man has been screwing our 16 year old daughter!"

"Well Ben you might want to stay calm because the worse has not been told yet." John knew that what he had to say next would put his buddy right over the edge. Before he could brace himself and prepare to tell the rest of what he'd heard Ben demanded, "What else is there John?"

"The man's name is Mitchell. I believe the man is your son in law."

Indiscretions of a Married Man

"What the hell did you just say John?" The walls seemed as though they were squeezing the life out of Ben as he heard the name of the man.

"Ben, I overheard Monica tell Debra his wife was out of town and she made a mistake and called his wife's name ... she called her Andrea, Debra stopped her in her tracks, calling her on it."

"John you're kidding me. If this is true that mother fucker will rot in a jail cell!"

Helen began to process what they had just heard from John and she wasn't quite sure how to react. She went numb. "Ben what about Andrea, how could Monica do this to her sister?"

"Where is Monica? She needs to get her ass here!" Ben could not get the sentence out of his mouth fast enough. He could not even imagine what he just heard. He hoped it was not true but the gut of his stomach told him it was true. One thing he knew was that Mitchell was about to pay for what he had done. Ben walked towards the phone and looked over at his wife Helen. Her head hung low, tears rolling down her face. He could not stand the thought of his wife crying about anything. He had done his best over the past 35 years to keep her as happy as he could because she deserved it and now this sorry bastard had come into their life and devastated their entire family. Why? Because he couldn't keep his dick in his pants, well he would be so damn sorry Ben promised his wife. He quickly glanced at John who was not saying much more. I guess he realized he had said more than enough for one night, no for one

49

Indiscretions of a Married Man

lifetime. Ben picked up the phone not realizing the tears welling in his eyes. At first he felt as though he would explode but the anger slowly gave way to sadness, sadness for his oldest daughter. Andrea didn't deserve this and who has to tell her? Helen certainly is in no condition to tell her. Well, first things first. Ben picked up the phone and dialed 911. Helen and John were able to hear one side of the conversation, confirming the number Ben had dialed.

"I would like to report a crime."

"Yes, statutory rape."

"Yes ma'am, his name is Mitchell Reed."

Chapter 11

"I feel good today!" Well, I have to admit that every since Andrea has been back from her Biloxi trip things could not be any better. She is due back in tonight from New Orleans. She rode with Sharon, who was taking her daughter to visit the grandparents. The way she greeted me when she returned from Biloxi, how could I refuse her another weekend trip? Mitchell was so proud of how he had worked through his feeling of jealousy and possessiveness. He smiled at the thought that he had everything under control. For a moment he thought his world would be turned upside down but it seems as though all his worries were finally under the bridge. "Damn I can't wait until Andrea gets back tonight. Today is a good day and tonight is going to be alright!"

Mitchell drifted deeper into thought and was enjoying every minute of it before the intercom interrupted with Tonya's voice, "Mr. Reid."

"Yes Tonya, what is it?"

"There are two men in the lobby to see you."

"Do they have an appointment?"

"No sir, but they say it is urgent that they see you."

"Who are they Tonya? Have they given a name?"

"No, but one presented a detective badge."

"Okay, show them in." Mitchell wondered what in the hell they wanted.

As the door opened Tonya showed the two detectives in, Mitchell stood, extended his arm to shake each man's hand. "Gentlemen good afternoon, how can I be of help to you?"

"You are Mitchell Reid?" asked the smaller of the two men.

"Yes sir I am." Suddenly Mitchell was not feeling so elated.

"Mr. Reid I am Detective Jones and this is my partner Detective Calloway. We are here because we have a warrant for your arrest."

Excuse me Mr.... I mean Detective did you say *ugh* my arrest, a warrant? Are you sure you have the right person? Why would you have a warrant for my arrest?"

Indiscretions of a Married Man

"Well Mr. Reid if you would slow it down and give us a moment to respond we will read the charges."

Mitchell stood there not believing what he was hearing because he was so sure they had made the biggest mistake but the more he looked at their faces the more convinced he was that maybe this was not a mistake that could easily be fixed. "The charges that have been filed against you are statutory rape."

Mitchell began to relax a little because he was sure they had made a mistake. It was almost as if he slightly exhaled and nervously smiled as he spoke," Sir I am sure you have made a big mistake; I am definitely not a rapist. I have a wife!" Once he said wife his mind slowly opened up to what could have possibly brought the detectives to his door. Slowly he heard himself ask, "Who brought the charges?" Already knowing the answer before it ever reached the detectives lips.

"Mr. and Mrs. Brown have brought the charges against you Mr. Reid and we will need to read you your rights." Mitchell's head became light; his worst nightmare was now a reality. He saw lips moving but heard nothing. Finally Detective Calloway, the taller of the two detectives spoke. "Mr. Reid because we are at your place of business we can do this one of two ways if you are willing to cooperate. We can take you out in cuffs or we can allow you to walk out with us. The choice is yours."

Mitchell just stood there completely numb. "Mr. Reid, what's it going to be?"

Indiscretions of a Married Man

"Mr. Reid?" Detective Jones asked for the second time, trying not to be too hostile because it was apparent the man was in total shock.

Finally Mitchell came back and realized he was expected to answer. "*Ugh,* just let me put my jacket on, I'll cooperate. Please don't cuff me. I do have to return here once this is cleared up."

"No problem Mr. Reid. Follow us please."

As Mitchell slowly opened the office door he took a deep breath and stepped through it thanking God that only Tonya was in the lobby. "Tonya, please cancel any remaining appointments that I have scheduled for the day. I will be out for the rest of the afternoon."

"Mr. Reid is everything okay?" Tonya asked but could look at Mitchell's face and see that everything was not okay.

"Tonya everything is fine. I will call back to the office later in the day." Mitchell walked down the hall to the elevators between the two detectives, stepped on the elevator and rode to the first floor. The ride seemed to take forever. They stepped off of the elevator and walked to the front door of the office building, it seemed to take an eternity. What he dreaded most was getting into the back of the detective car. But when he thought it could get no worse Detective Jones turned to the back seat and said, "we will need to cuff you now Mr. Reid." Mitchell placed both hands out and watched as they placed the silver bracelets around his wrists. He sat back in the seat and thought to himself it was only an hour ago that he was in the comfort zone of his office entertaining the thought of making love to his wife when she returned… With that thought Mitchell's heart began to ache, tears slipped out of his eyes as he heard himself whisper, "Oh Andrea I am so, so sorry!"

Chapter 12

"It is so good to be home." Andrea sighed as Sharon pulled up into her driveway.

"Your house looks pretty dark girl. Where's that man of yours?" Sharon asked.

"Well he's expecting me in and it's about what time?"

"The time is 9:45 P.M. Do you know where your man is?" Sharon always had jokes; you had to laugh at her because they were always funny and her facial expressions didn't make it much better.

"Okay Sharon, don't start with the jokes. You've done so well the entire trip. We get back home and you just have to start with your shit." Andrea had grown to really appreciate Sharon's friendship. She had a great respect for all she represented.

"Lighten up Andrea, just joking with you sister."

Indiscretions of a Married Man

"I know girl, I know. Mitchell's probably gone to bed thinking he's about to get the Biloxi treatment, uh, not tonight." They both laughed at the thought.

"Now you know you're going to give that man that Biloxi treat, that's probably why he was so easy about you going with me to New Orleans. You know men girl, they will do whatever it takes for some lock jaw."

I began to laugh at Sharon because she said exactly what I was thinking when Mitchell took it so easy about my going with her to New Orleans.

"You're laughing because it's true isn't it, ha I know it is." Sharon laughed as I got out of her car.

"I will see you at work tomorrow."

"Yeah you are right about that, wish I didn't have to show. Hey sister, thanks for coming along."

"Thanks for having me."

As Andrea entered the house and closed the door she suddenly became exhausted. After checking the house she realized that Mitchell hadn't gotten in yet so she stretched out on the sofa in the den with the intent of watching a little television. She began to flick through the channels and thought, "it's a damn shame to have so many channels on cable and still nothing on worth watching." She finally turned to channel 55, Lifetime, Television for woman, "That's just what I need right about now." Andrea laughed at herself as she tried to figure out what was going on in the movie. She hated

Indiscretions of a Married Man

tuning in to a movie that was in the middle of being over, although the movie seemed pretty good. But weren't all lifetime movies pretty good? Of course it would be about some man abusing, cheating or killing his wife. Andrea stretched out and relaxed, within 15 minutes she was comfortably sleeping with the television watching her. After what seemed to be a few minutes of the best nap she'd taken in a while, Andrea was awaken by the low ringing of the phone. She slowly opened her eyes in an attempt to acclimate herself of her surroundings. As she pulled her thoughts together she realized that she was still on the couch. Andrea glanced at the clock on the wall noting that the time was 3:47 a.m. "I can't believe I've been asleep for over four hours. It only seemed like a couple of minutes. I must have been awfully tired for Mitchell to leave me on the couch." Andrea dragged herself off of the couch, wanting to get up the stairs and in the bed with her husband. He's too damn considerate lately. Andrea smiled to herself as she climbed the stairs. She walked into their bedroom, not turning on any lights to wake him. The streetlight shone dimly through the bedroom window allowing you to see shadows and hues. As her vision adjusted to the darkness in their bedroom she noticed that there was no shadow of Mitchell's body in their bed. Andrea reached for the light switch to confirm what her eyes told her. Once turning on the light, she saw no evidence of Mitchell being there. Immediately Andrea began to get angry.

Indiscretions of a Married Man

Maybe Mitchell did not take her going to New Orleans with Sharon this weekend too well. That surely was no reason to stay out all night. He never stayed out all night, the man rarely went out. Andrea sat on the edge of the bed trying to contain her anger. Deciding that she would handle Mitchell in the morning, Andrea pulled the blanket back, got in the bed, covered herself up and turned the light out, refusing to be up the rest of the morning worrying about him. Andrea had gotten so caught up in the reasoning of why her husband was not home at 3:47 in the morning that she totally forgot about the ringing of the phone that initially woke her.

Chapter 13

Andrea was awakened by the tweets of the birds; she quickly glanced at the clock noting it was 7:30 in the morning. She then looked to the other side of the bed and her anger immediately returned at the realization that Mitchell had not come home last night. Andrea began to feel an anxiety attack coming on. She did not know what to do or who to call.

Before she left for New Orleans things seemed to be going well between her and Mitchell so she really did not understand what was going on right now. Mitchell had never spent the night out

Indiscretions of a Married Man

regardless of any problems they may have had in the past. Andrea peeled the covers back and began to get out of the bed trying not to think about where he was or whom he was with. She began to walk down the hall and then turned around and returned to the bed. She sat down on the edge of the bed and slowly the reality that her husband had spent the night outside of their home settled in. Tears began to find their way down Andrea's face as she slumped deeper into the bed.

    As sobs began to rack her body the phone rang. She was sobbing so loudly that it took her a minute to hear the phone. She reached for the phone and tried to pull herself together so that whoever was on the other end of the phone would not detect the pain and anger she was feeling now. She picked the phone up after the third ring and a recorded voice immediately began to speak in her ear, "This is a collect call from an inmate at a correction facility…." Trying to compose herself to make sure she heard the recorded voice correctly, she caught the last bit of the recording "... to accept these charges please press 1." Not sure who was calling collect from jail, the first thought that came to Andrea's mind was that this was Mitchell and this explained why he had not come home last night. He had probably been pulled over for something so simple. She quickly pressed one and sure enough after the automated voice said thank you, it was Mitchell's voice. "Andrea?"

She slowly exhaled as she asked, "Mitchell, what are you doing in jail? I was so worried when you didn't come home last night.

Indiscretions of a Married Man

What's going on baby?" Andrea began to feel better knowing that Mitchell had a legitimate excuse for not coming home. Mitchell did not know how to explain to his wife the reason he was in jail. One thing he knew for sure was that he could not explain to her over the phone. He thought about this call all night and still had not come up with any way to ease the pain this situation was about to bring to his wife. "Baby, I need for you to come…please…" Mitchell's voice trembled and he became very soft spoken, trying to contain his voice from completely breaking down. Andrea detected something wrong in her husband's voice but she credited it to him being in jail. "Baby I'll be there. Where are you? Have they given you a bail or bond?" Andrea had no clue of what she was supposed to do but she would call the jail after she hung up and get the details she needed.

"I'm in Dekalb County. I don't have a bond yet. I believe I have to go before the Judge." Mitchell knew he wouldn't be getting a bond until he saw the Judge. Hopefully that would be today. He didn't want to tell Andrea that because then she would ask more questions that he was not prepared to answer just yet.

"Baby, Do I need to call a bondsman or something?" Andrea asked but before he could answer her, the automated voice entered the conversation," This call is from an inmate in a correction facility…." It's no wonder he sounds the way he does Andrea thought, hell he's humiliated. All she could think of was getting to the jail and getting her husband out.

Indiscretions of a Married Man

"No baby, I think I have to go before the Judge first. I'm not even sure if they will let you come down here and see me." Mitchell answered hoping the interruption distracted his wife's line of questioning.

"Baby, what happen?" Andrea asked, realizing that she still didn't know why Mitchell was in jail.

"Andrea, please baby let's talk about it when you get here."

"Okay baby I'm on my way."

"Okay. Andrea I..." before he could finish the sentence the phone disconnected. The rest of his sentence went uncompleted in his wife's ear but he finished the sentence anyway, "...love you."

Andrea held the phone to her ear as it went dead in her hand. She hung the phone up and sat for a minute to get her thoughts together. She then picked the phone back up and began to dial the number to the county jail. The phone seemed to ring forever before someone actually answered. "Dekalb County jail, how may I direct your call?"

"Sir, I am calling to find out what the charges are on my husband and how much it will be to bail him out?" Andrea asked nervously.

"What is the name ma'am?"

"His name is Mitchell Reid."

"And when was he brought in?"

"I believe it was sometime last night."

Indiscretions of a Married Man

"Please hold, it will be a minute, our computer is a little slow this morning."

As Andrea waited to hear the charges, she was becoming impatient, wanting the sheriff on the other end to give her the information she needed so that she could get to the bank and the bondsman to get her husband out so that they could put this little episode behind them. After what seemed like forever the sheriff's voice returned, "Ma'am, he is charged with statutory rape.

"Sir, there must be a mistake. I said his name is Mitchell Reid, my husband, Mitchell Reid!"

"No Mrs. Reid, I don't believe it is a mistake, we only have one Mitchell Reid here, now unless your husband is in another county, those are his charges."

"Is there anything more I can help you with?" The sheriff asked, feeling sorry for the woman on the other end of the phone. He could tell from her voice that she was not taking the charges well at all. "No sir, thank you." Long after the sheriff disconnected the call, Andrea held the phone to her ear. She was in total shock. It seemed as though a ton of bricks had just fallen on her heart. As Andrea sat on the edge of the bed, she couldn't think, she didn't know who to talk to because this was something she couldn't dare tell anyone. Convinced there was more to this than she could see, Andrea began to get dressed as she convinced herself that this was a mistake and Mitchell would be able to explain it. The bond was so high. They didn't have that kind of money and besides the sheriff

Indiscretions of a Married Man

said it had to be a property bond. She thought about her parents. They owned their home, but she didn't want to involve them until she was sure of what the hell was going on. Andrea was completely dressed and heading for the door when the phone rang. "Damn, who in the hell is calling this early?" Andrea picked up the phone without checking the caller id. "Hello."

"Hey baby. How are you doing?" Her dad asked very softly almost in a whisper.

Andrea thought to herself that she could not talk to her father or her mom until she got this shit straight with Mitchell. "Hey dad, I'm okay but I really don't have time to talk right now. I'll call you when I get in this evening."

"Andrea, I really need to talk to you as soon as possible I can be there in twenty minutes." Ben wondered why his daughter seemed calm but hurried. He was sure she had to know by now that her husband was in jail for rape and he had not heard from her since yesterday. He had begun to worry and that is what prompted his call.

"Dad please don't, I have to go I'll call you when I get home." Andrea hung the phone up before her father could say anything more. She hurried out the door and got into her jeep. As she started the engine and prepared to back out of the driveway, tears began to roll down her face. Andrea sniffled and before long she was crying so hard it wracked her body. She must have sat in the driveway with the engine running for twenty minutes before she was able to gain control and pull off. Heading toward the jail, Andrea said out loud to herself, "Damn, I guess I needed that."

Chapter 14

"She knows." Ben said to his wife as he hung the phone up.

"Ben I don't think she knows the entire truth." Helen said.

"Baby, she knows! I can hear it in her voice."

"You do not have to yell Ben. This is devastating to the entire family not just you." In all the years they had been together, Helen had never seen her husband in this state. He was emotionally torn apart. Last night she thought he was going to seriously hurt their younger daughter, Monica.

Monica came home shortly after John left. She walked in the door as though she had not done a thing. She was heading up the stairs toward her room when Ben called, "Monica, come in here right now." At first he seemed to be very calm.

"...In a minute Dad." Monica said.

"Not in a minute. I said right now and that is what I mean!"

"What is his problem?" Monica said as she strolled into the den.

Indiscretions of a Married Man

I was sitting in the chair with my head in my hands wondering what my youngest daughter could have been thinking. As Monica entered the den her mother looked up at her with tear stained eyes.

"What is going on mom? Is there something wrong?" Monica asked. *Monica was beginning to look worried from the tears in her mother's eyes and the look on her father's face. Her father told her to have a seat. She had never seen her parents like this before. Her father stared at her for a long while before he said anything.*

"Monica, John was over here this evening and he told us something that was so shocking. I refuse to believe what he told us has any truth." *Ben knew in his heart it was true but he still hoped that there had been some sort of mistake in what John overheard.*

"What is it Dad?" *Monica immediately thought something had happened to Debra.*

"John says he overheard you telling his daughter that you had sex with an older man and that the man is Mitchell. Now Monica, I need for you to tell me that John doesn't know what he's talking about or that he misunderstood." *Her father stared at her as though he was looking through her. You could almost see Monica's heart miss a beat. She couldn't believe this was happening to her. She was so afraid of what her father was going to do. She opened her mouth but the words would not drop out.*

"Say something! Open your damn mouth and say something right now!" *Ben's voice began to quickly go from calm to a scream. Helen looked at him in shock.* "Ben please, honey you have got to calm down."

"Calm down my ass! Helen, do you not realize what she has done?" *Ben was quickly losing control and Monica had fear written across her face.* "You have one minute to answer the damn question or so help me God I am going to knock the hell out of you tonight!" *Ben yelled as he began to get up from his seat.*

"Daddy, I didn't say...."

"Don't you lie to me girl!" *Ben began to walk towards her. Helen finally spoke because Ben was not handling this well. Helen wasn't either but yelling at her wasn't going to erase what had happened.*

"Monica, please tell us what happened, all we want to know is how did this happen."

"What happened is that she has been sleeping with her sister's husband!" *Ben yelled.*

"Ben please, calm down."

"Calm down? I'll calm down!" *Ben stood directly in front of Monica ready to yank her out of the chair. She looked scared to death.*

Indiscretions of a Married Man

"Daddy, I'm sorry. It just happened. I don't know how it happened, it just did. I went over there to watch a movie and he came home and it just happened..." Monica said in a small voice. Helen knew she was lying and so did Ben.

"Well that sorry son of a bitch is going to rot in jail if I have anything to do with it!" Ben said, trying to calm himself, not knowing what to do with her.

"How could you do that to your sister Monica? How...?" Helen asked her. She just sat there and stared like her mother had said nothing. Ben demanded an answer from her and she replied, "She's not perfect, she's done things to me." Before Monica could say another word her father reared his hand back and slapped her across the face twice. I jumped from my seat and grabbed him before he swung a third time. "Ben, please."
Monica sat in the chair; her body trembling with tears pouring down her face. Between the sobs she cried, "I'm sorry, I'm so sorry."

"You're not sorry yet! First thing in the morning you will tell your sister exactly what you did! That's when you will be sorry! The sight of you makes me sick." Ben walked out of the den never looking back.

Ben seemed to be a lot calmer this morning and Monica had not come out of her room since last night. One thing Helen knew for certain was that this nightmare had just begun and once it was over this family would never be the same.

Indiscretions of a Married Man

Chapter 15

Andrea stood in the lobby waiting for her name to be called from the visitor log. She was not sure what the outcome of this visit would be but one thing she was sure of was that she would walk away from here with the truth. She was jolted out of her thoughts as her name was called. Andrea was then directed down a long corridor that had little rooms on both sides of the hall. Each room had a letter followed by a number above the door. The doors had small windows you could look through. As Andrea passed each door, she glanced in. Some rooms were empty while others had someone seated waiting for their visitor. Andrea was given a security badge with D5 on the front of it, which was at the end of the corridor. Once she stepped inside the room she noticed the sheet of glass that separated visitor from inmate. There was a stool and phone on each side of the glass. Andrea sat down and waited for her husband to appear on the other side of the glass. Within minutes Mitchell stood in front of her in an orange jumpsuit. He quietly took his seat. The sight of him made Andrea smile and Mitchell tried to return the smile although he knew that before this visit was over neither one of them would be smiling. Andrea and Mitchell sat on opposite sides of the glass staring at each other. Each wondering what should be

Indiscretions of a Married Man

said. Andrea spoke first, "Baby, tell me what's going on here." Mitchell continued to stare as Andrea cleared her throat for the questioning to come. "Mitchell, what's going on?" Andrea asked with knots twisting in her stomach. Mitchell whispered so softly that the words could not be heard. It seemed as though his mouth was moving but no sound came out. Andrea waited for his response but he said nothing. He just continued to stare at her with sadness in his eyes. She had never seen her husband look this way before. On her way to the jail she had convinced herself that there was a simple explanation for all of this but now sitting across from her husband looking at him she began to feel very unsure. It was apparent that Mitchell was not in a very talkative mood nor was he spitting out any answers so Andrea pulled her emotions together and began questioning. "Mitchell I called the jail before I left home so that everything would be in place for me to bond you out once I got here but they said the bond was $150 thousand dollars and that I need a property bond." Andrea waited for him to respond, still nothing so she continued. "Do you know what your charges are?" He opened his mouth to speak but nothing came out. He didn't know how to handle this or what to say to her because if he told her the truth he might not ever see his wife again. He could not bear the thought of losing his wife while in jail. Therefore to prevent that from occurring he decided he would say no more than he needed to. His defense was innocent until proven guilty. He refused to admit guilt because he had too much to lose. Even if he wanted to explain he

Indiscretions of a Married Man

couldn't because it would tear his wife apart. He didn't know how to tell her why he was there without inflicting so much pain so he just stared at her.

"Mitchell, I asked you do you know what your charges are."

"Yes. I've been told what they are." He whispered.

"And…." Andrea was beginning to get a little irritated at her husband as he continued to stare and say nothing. "And Mitchell what is this about?!" Andrea repeated.

"You already know what the charges are." He could not bring himself to say the charges to his wife.

"I want you to tell me what the charge is and then I want you to tell me this is a very big mistake Mitchell."

"Andrea, please not now."

"What is the charge Mitchell?" Andrea tried to remain calm because of where they were.

"The charge is statutory Rape." He barely whispered.

"Are these charges true?"

"Andrea please this is not the time for…"

"This is not the time for what? For you to tell me how you have ended up in jail with a charge of statutory rape!" Andrea suddenly began to feel all of her strength slowly seeping from her body and she began to plead, "Mitchell, please baby, just tell me what is going on. Help me understand what's happening here. Please." Tears began to swell up in Andrea's eyes and as they rolled down her face Mitchell opened his mouth to speak but no words

Indiscretions of a Married Man

would come out. He couldn't find any words that would stop his wife from crying. As he watched the tears roll down her face his heart ached because he knew that once he opened his mouth to explain, the words would rip her heart right out of her chest. He just couldn't bring himself to do that. He would rather her assume than to have to witness that. As he stared at her through the glass he wished he could turn back the hands of time. One moment of weakness had cost him more than he could ever have imagined and he was sure he wasn't finished paying yet.

Andrea realized that this visit was going nowhere. Mitchell was not talking and it was too emotionally stressful for her to continue to sit in tears staring at her husband through a glass. "Maybe tomorrow will bring a better day". She said softly to herself as she stood up from the stool and touched the glass before turning and walking through the door. She walked quickly down the corridor never turning to look back.

As Mitchell watched his wife walk through the door in pain he realized that his moment of weakness had cost him his life. That was what Andrea was to him, his life. He knew he could not breathe without her. The thought of not having her in his life was unthinkable until now. He had traded it all for one weekend of sex, forbidden fruit. There was nothing he could do to ease her tears or pain. Once the entire truth came out, it would only worsen his wife's pain. Tears fell out of his eyes as he continued to sit on the other side of the glass and asked himself, "What have I done to my life and to my wife?" He stared at the door as if she would walk back through it but she never did.

Chapter 16

Andrea walked down the corridor towards the controlled exit and it seemed a much longer walk than when she came. She tried to focus her tear-blurred vision before she approached the sheriff patrolling the entrance and exit areas. She returned the badge to him and exited toward the parking lot. Once inside her Jeep Andrea sat without starting the engine, she wondered why she was more confused than before their visit. She was so sure that once their visit was over she would have felt better but as she sat in her car she felt worse and she still had no answers. Andrea did not know where to begin to reason this out. She could not find the beginning or the end and she began to convince herself Mitchell was in as much shock as she was and he needed time to focus before answering questions. He just needed a little time. Her husband just was not that type of man. She could not even entertain the thought of statutory rape. No way, not her man there was just no way. She would just have to wait until she bonded him out and then they could work on figuring out what the hell happen here. As she continued to sit in her jeep she did realize that they had no property bond, they were buying their house

Indiscretions of a Married Man

but they did not own it yet and they did not have $150 thousand dollars. This sure was a fine mess her husband had gotten himself into but once they got this shit resolved everything would be fine, "Everything will be fine," Andrea repeated out loud trying to convince her that it would be just that. She wanted her husband home today and the only help she could think of was her parents. As much as Andrea tried to keep her parents out of her business this was one time she was going to have to place her pride aside and ask for their help. Her dad had never been too fond of Mitchell but over the years he had learned to tolerate him. Andrea assumed that it was because her dad just didn't think anyone was good enough for her. She started the engine and drove toward her parent's house, wanting to get this over with and her husband home so that they could get this resolved. "What a big fucking mistake the county has made!" Andrea said aloud as an afterthought of a lawsuit appeared in her mind. While driving she tried to conceive a way to avoid telling her parents the charge. Her dad would insist on knowing the charges once she told him what the county was requiring for her husband to be free. She continued to think and realized that once she explained this mess her dad would support her and not give her a hard time. Deep in her heart she knew she was his favorite and that there was nothing he wouldn't do for her. She pulled into her parent's driveway preparing herself for her dad's speech but also for him signing that property bond so that she could get her husband home and they could get this mess worked out and behind them.

Indiscretions of a Married Man

Chapter 17

Andrea braced herself as she approached her parent's front door. Before she could ball her hand up to knock, the door opened, as she entered her parent's home she noticed the look on her dad's face and thought to herself, "He knows."

"Hey daddy..." Andrea said.

"Hey baby, I'm glad you decided to come by." Ben said as he dreaded what was to come. He realized it was his duty as a father to handle this situation regardless of how much pain it was about to unleash.

"Where's Mom? I need to talk with you both."

"She is upstairs but I will call her down. We need to talk with you as well."

"Well daddy, I came by because Mitchell and I have a situation and we need your help."

Just the sound of Mitchell's name passing through his daughter's lips made Ben's entire body tense and it did not get pass Andrea's eyes. She assumed that her dad tensed because he was not very fond of Mitchell therefore she continued to speak, after all she

Indiscretions of a Married Man

was on a mission and that mission was to get her husband out of jail today! Andrea thought that taking a deep breath and then just blurting the entire situation out would make it easy. So that is what she did, "Dad, Mitchell is jail. The bond is $150 thousand dollars and they want a property bond. Now daddy I know you are not too fond of Mitchell but if you could put that aside and help us out here I would appreciate it so much." Andrea took a deep breath after saying all of that.

Ben did not know how to approach this situation. As he looked into her face his heart felt so heavy for his oldest daughter because he could see the belief she had in her husband was so sincere. He realized that his daughter did not have a clue as to why her husband was in jail. Ben did not want to be the one to tell her, he just did not want to be the one exposing the pain that was to come. Monica was in her room but he was about to bring her out of her comfort zone so that she could be accountable for her mess. No one else should have to take on the job of explaining her mess. He walked toward the steps to call for his wife and his daughter.

"Baby, why don't you go into the den and sit while I get your mother."

"Okay dad, I just want you to know that once Mitchell and I get this mess cleared up you will not have lost anything." Andrea said trying to reassure her dad that the risk he was taking would only be a temporary one. As Ben reached the middle of the hall he called for his wife, Helen. He began to walk up the steps heading toward

Indiscretions of a Married Man

Monica's bedroom door. He reached to turn the doorknob to open the door, summoning his youngest daughter down the stairs but as he began to turn the doorknob he decided that he still could not look at her. He released the doorknob and called her name through the door ordering her downstairs to the den. Before she could respond by opening the door Ben had already turned and was heading down the stairs in disgust.

Monica was not sure why her dad was requesting her presence downstairs. Every since that night he had not even spoken her name, less on look at her. She assumed they wanted to make sure she had not forgotten what she had done. She had been in her room for what seemed like forever trying to avoid another confrontation but it was apparent that her strategy had ran out as of today. Monica slowly came down the stairs trying to prepare for the next episode, but once she got to the entrance of the den, she saw Andrea sitting on the sofa. Monica was not prepared for this. Her mother was seated in the recliner looking more composed than she had a couple of nights ago. Her father had placed himself by the door. Monica entered the den very slowly.

"Dad please tell me, why you are making this into a family meeting. This is my personal business and Monica has nothing to do with it." Andrea said as she wondered why her father thought it necessary to involve Monica.

Indiscretions of a Married Man

"Andrea please just sit there, your sister has something she needs to say to you." Ben felt a little better now that he did not have to be the bearer of the bad news to come.

"Okay dad but couldn't it wait for another time." Andrea just wanted the signature so that she could get her husband out of jail.

"No Andrea it cannot wait. Now open your mouth Monica and start talking." Ben said. As always Helen just sat as the silent partner only speaking to maintain order.

"What is it Monica? Please hurry because I have other business to attend to with mom and dad."
Monica just looked at her sister; she knew she could not do this. As much as she despised Andrea at times she could not do this to her sister so she sat and silently stared.

"You better open your mouth and start talking right now. You weren't so quiet when you were bragging to Debra, now open your damn mouth!"
Andrea began to get a little worried about what was going on here. This was not a normal family practice. "Dad what's going on here?" Andrea then looked into Monica's eyes and she suddenly knew what this was. Just as quickly as the thought crossed her mind is as quickly as she crossed it out with denial. There was no way that this could have anything to do with why her husband was in jail. But the more she looked into Monica's eyes the more she could not deny the fact. Andrea felt as though the room was closing in on her. She was afraid of what Monica might say. After taking a few minutes to

Indiscretions of a Married Man

absorb what was actually happening she opened her mouth to speak, "Monica what is it you need to say to me?" Monica continued to look at her older sister. All eyes were on her and she wanted them off. Andrea couldn't tell whether what she saw in her sister's eyes was fear or pain. What she was sure of was that it was something that she had not ever seen there before. "Monica, please say what you have to say."

Monica opened her mouth and softly spoke her sister's name, *"Andrea...I am so sorry."* A stream of tears flowed down Monica's face.

"What do you mean you're sorry? You're sorry for what Monica? Why are you crying? What is going on here?" Andrea asked in a panic.

Monica felt like a trapped animal. She never imagined what she and Mitchell did would come to this. It had caused so much pain to other people. It was just suppose to be sex, just a good time. "What went wrong?" she asked herself quietly as she rose from her seat. She was ready to exit the room not able to stand any more of the pressure. Before she could stand good enough to take the first step her father was standing in front of her.

"Where in the hell do you think you're going?" He asked.

Monica said nothing as her father shoved her back into her seat. Andrea stared in a daze at her father's aggressiveness. For as long as she could remember he had never laid a hand on either of them. Monica sunk back into her seat as her body convulsed with sobs.

Indiscretions of a Married Man

Realizing that this was about to become a repeat of the last time, Helen stepped in. Helen knew there was no easy way to tell her oldest daughter that her husband had slept with her younger sister so she decided to be direct and to the point. That was how she handled everything and this could be no exception. "Andrea baby, we know about Mitchell being in jail and we are aware that the charge is statutory rape. Your dad... we had him arrested for sleeping with Monica while you were in Biloxi..."

The room began to spin as Andrea moved in slow motion. She stood to get away from what her mother had just said. She walked toward Monica in total disbelief. She felt as though she had stepped outside of herself. She opened her mouth to speak but was choked by her own sobbing, "Monica, please say no, please tell me it's not true..."

Monica looked at her sister standing in front of her and there was absolutely nothing she could say to Andrea. She would never forgive herself for the pain she saw in her sister's face. She had never seen her sister in this state and it tore her apart to know that she was the cause of it. Monica lowered her head into her hands not able to look her sister in her face. All Monica could say was, "I'm sorry Andrea."

Andrea looked Monica in the eyes and thought of what she was hearing. It was slowly registering that her husband was in jail because he slept with her sixteen-year-old sister. They had sex. Where did they do it? Why did they do it? She realized that her

Indiscretions of a Married Man

husband's charge of statutory rape was correct, it was no mistake. Anger began to seep in and Andrea called her sister's name, "Monica! Monica!" Monica lifted her head from her hands and looked up at Andrea. Andrea reached back and slapped Monica as hard as she could. "How could you do this to me? You're my sister. You're supposed to love me! Why Monica? Why?" Andrea cried as she crumbled to the floor at her sister's feet. It was then that Ben stepped in and he reached down and lifted Andrea's limp body off of the floor carrying her down the hall into the guestroom. He gently laid her down on the bed, cradling her in his arms as she cried, "How could she do this to me daddy? How could they do it?" Ben could say nothing because he had no answer for what had happened. He rocked his daughter in his arms attempting to make the pain vanish. As he cradled her in his arms, he wanted to say something to comfort his daughter, to make her feel better but he was so choked up on his own tears of pain, he could say nothing. Her pain had become his pain, her tears his tears.

Chapter 18

Andrea awakened in her father's arms, incoherent for a brief moment. Her head pulsated and her body felt as though someone had stomped all over it. As she began to stir in her father's arms he

Indiscretions of a Married Man

loosened his hold on her and quietly asked was she all right and did she need anything. Instantly the day's events came flooding back to her. She felt the tears forming in her eyes again and was determined to blink them away. "No, I'm fine daddy. I've got to get up from here and take care of a few things." Andrea's voice trembled and her father knew she was not okay but he did not want to push her into another emotional breakdown.

"What time is it?" Her father glanced at his watch surprised that they had slept through the night. "Baby it is 9:30 in the morning."

"You have to be joking. Dad, I slept straight through the night?"

"Yes baby and you needed it. Sometimes rest is the best comforter." Ben had learned that from earlier years of experience.

Andrea moved out of her father arms and stretched as she rose from the bed. She stood still for a moment, preparing to leave. She straightened herself out as she exited the guestroom, heading toward the front door. Andrea turned and gave her father a long hug.

"Tell mom I said goodbye dad." Andrea said not wanting to stay in her parent's house any longer than she had to.

"I believe she stepped out early this morning for her doctor's appointment."

"Dad, just tell her I said I love her and I'll call later."

"Okay then baby. Are you sure you're alright?" Ben asked as he opened the front door to let her out. Andrea walked down the driveway toward her jeep; she began to think of how empty she felt. She was confused because she had no answers. She needed some type of explanation before she left from her parent's house today and the one person who could give her that was upstairs. Andrea turned around and looked at her father.

"No Dad I'm not alright. I need to talk to Monica. I need for her to tell me what happened while I was in Biloxi. Where is she?"

"She is in her room. Are you sure you want to do that baby?" Ben asked realizing this could be another scene that he really had no energy for.

"I'm sure dad. I have to do this."

"Well I will be outside cutting this grass before it gets too hot, call me if you need me."

Andrea began to walk up the stairs. She knocked lightly on Monica's door and before Monica could ask who was knocking, Andrea opened the door and stepped inside the room. Monica was laid across her bed on her back staring at the ceiling until the door opened. Seeing Andrea standing in the doorway Monica suddenly sat up. They stared at each other for a brief moment before Monica lowered her eyes.

"Monica, we need to talk." Andrea said as she closed the door behind her. Monica knew this was coming but had not anticipated it coming this quickly. Andrea sat down in the lazy boy facing her.

"I want you to tell me what happened, Monica. I want to know how you and my husband ended up in my bed." Andrea felt pretty calm considering what she might hear.

Indiscretions of a Married Man

"Andrea it just happened." Monica hoped her answer would kill this conversation.

"Sleeping with your sister's husband isn't something that just happens! You can't think of anything better than "*it just happened*". Bullshit, it didn't just happen! I don't plan on leaving this room until you tell me what happened while I was gone. You can either tell me voluntarily or I will beat the shit out of you but one way or the other you are going to tell me how your ass ended up in the bed with my husband!" Andrea stood up and walked toward the bedroom door locking it. "Now what's it going to be?"

Monica stared at Andrea in disbelief. She always felt that her sister was a pushover. All talk, no action, but she became a little nervous after watching her sister lock the door. She truly believed her sister would beat her ass in this room today. She took a deep breath and began to explain her version…

"I went over to your house to watch some cable, like you said I could. Mitchell wasn't home when I got there. I sat in the den and watched "If Loving You Is Wrong" on OWN, trying to catch up on the episodes I missed this season on "On Demand". I must have fallen asleep before the movie ended. I woke up when I heard the front door opening. It was Mitchell. I guess he was just getting in from work, it was pretty late. He came in the den to see who was watching the television. He called your name and I guess he thought I was you. When he saw it was me, he came over and sat down next to me on the couch. He started to complain about the things that

were wrong in your marriage." Monica hesitated, trying to pull her story together.

"Is that when you decided fucking him would make him feel better?" Andrea could feel herself getting angry once again.

"No I did not invite your husband to have sex with me; he's the one who came on to me!" Monica said as she began to get on the defense, sick of this whole situation. She definitely was not in the mood for her sister's smart-ass attitude.

"He came on to you and you're such a trick that you didn't know how to get your ass up and go home? Or even say no for that matter!"

"Don't get ugly with me because your husband couldn't keep his dick in his pants!" Once Monica said it she knew she couldn't take it back. She felt bad about what happened but she was not going to take all the blame. Andrea stood in front of her like her husband was a saint. Well he wasn't and she needed to wake up and realize that.

"Excuse me, what the hell did you just say?" Andrea walked up on her sister daring her to repeat it.

"You heard what I said Andrea, your man ain't no saint!" This was the perfect time to bring her sister down a few notches.

"So that gives you the okay to fuck him! Are you so jealous of me that you would sleep with my husband? Everything I've ever had you have always wanted, but to sleep with Mitchell, Monica…"

Indiscretions of a Married Man

"Don't get it twisted sis, it was the other way around, he wanted me! It's not my fault if you can't hold your man." Monica wanted to knock Andrea off of her high horse.

"You trifling trick!" Andrea shouted as she swung with every ounce of strength left in her and smacked Monica in the mouth. Before Monica could react Andrea had knocked her down and was on top of her throwing continuous blows. Monica tried to get up but her sister's weight pinned her down. She managed to reach up and get in one blow skimming Andrea's jaw line. It was that one blow that snapped Andrea back. She looked down at her sister and her sister looked up at her with a busted lip, bloodied nose and a quickly swelling red eye that would be black by morning. Andrea still did not feel sorry for Monica. She was actually disgusted with her. She rose off her and spit in her face, "Trick bitch!" she said as she walked out of her sister's room, down the steps toward the front door. As she opened the front door, she heard her younger sister whimpering from upstairs and her father asking was everything okay from the front yard. "Yes dad everything is just fine and getting better." Andrea smiled as she closed the front door. She felt better than she had in three days. She thought about how pitiful her sister was. Monica pretended to be so remorseful in front of their parents but when she was behind the closed door she showed her true self. "And that is why I beat her ass like a trick in the street. One thing is for damn sure Monica will think twice before she talks shit to me again." Andrea said out loud as she traveled

Indiscretions of a Married Man

home. She had called out from work for the remainder of the week…a family emergency. They understood.

Pulling into her driveway Andrea prepared herself for the next step. Packing Mitchell's shit and moving it into the garage for him to pick up. Andrea entered the house, closing the door behind her and she stood in the foyer staring at the den. She imagined her sixteen-year old sister and her husband wrapped nakedly around each other. "Did he make love to her the way he does me?" Andrea whimpered aloud. She began to cry for herself as she slowly walked into the den remembering. Remembering how she had made love to Mitchell the night she returned from Biloxi. Remembering how wonderful their relationship was going after her trip. Remembering the look in his eyes when he repeatedly told her he loved her. And then she remembered how Mitchell and Monica acted as though nothing had happened between them, they acted as though they had not spent the night together in her house...fucking! With that final thought, anger rose from the pit of Andrea's gut and she slammed the vase off the table down to the floor, the lamp from the table to the floor, anything that was in her reach was knocked down in a fury. As she ranted through the house she called Mitchell and Monica every name she could think of. Tearing his clothes from the hangers and destroying everything in her path. This went on for two hours before she began to feel drained. She lay down on her bed staring out of the window for what seemed like forever and although

Indiscretions of a Married Man

she was angry and determined not to feel sorry for herself the tears quietly streamed down her face until she drifted off to sleep.

Andrea slept completely through the night, awakening late the next morning. She slowly dragged herself up from the bed and headed towards the bathroom. She looked around at the mess she had created yesterday in her fit of rage. "Damn I fucked up a lot of shit." After using the bathroom, Andrea turned on the stereo and began jamming Boney James "Seduction"; she then opened a bottle of Chardonnay. Andrea's pity party was over. As Andrea sipped on her wine she began to pick up the broken pieces of everything scattered throughout the house. It took her most of the day to clean up the mess. Once she got the house back in order she began to pack Mitchell's things, placing them in boxes and stacking them against a wall in the garage. She knew that she was not ready to visit Mitchell just yet but she would soon have to visit and hear his version of what happen. She believed that her sister had mixed lies with the truth but she couldn't tell where the truth ended or the lie began. As Andrea continued to sip her wine she began to feel lonely. She wanted to talk to someone about what she was going through. She decided to call Sharon. As she listened to the ringing of the phone on the other end she realized that her family and her marriage would never be the same. Andrea wasn't sure how she and her husband would find their way back from this fucked up situation. Just as she was about to hang up the phone, Sharon picked up, "Hello."

"Hello, Sharon are you busy?"

Indiscretions of a Married Man

"No girl, why what's up? You don't sound too well."

"I'm okay I just needed to talk to somebody."

"Well I'm all ears and by the way why have you not been to work for the last couple of days. Where have you been?"

"I've been here Sharon, at home. I just needed a little time to pull it together, you know what I mean?"

As Sharon listened to her friend's choppy answer she realized something was truly wrong and that maybe she should get over there and physically check on her. "Hey I'm pretty damn bored here, you feel like some company?"

"Sure, I thought you would never ask."

"I'll pick up a bottle of something and be there in thirty."

"Okay. Sharon…"

"Yeah girl…"

"Thanks."

"That's what friends are for sister. See you in a minute."

Andrea sat on the couch awaiting her friend's knock. She wondered what she would say to Sharon. She didn't want Sharon to think Mitchell was a dog, she just wanted her friend to listen to how she felt without responding too much but she knew that was bullshit. Sharon was very vocal especially when it came to man issues. As she continued to sip and think, the doorbell rang. Andrea anxiously walked to the door in anticipation of her friend's company. She opened the door and welcomed Sharon in with a warm, needy hug.

Indiscretions of a Married Man

"Andrea, are you okay?" Sharon asked as she eased out of her friend's embrace.

"Yeah, I'm okay." Andrea tried to sound convincing but as she stood before her friend, she realized she was not as okay as she thought. Her voice began to tremble and tears followed. "Really I'm okay," Andrea sniffled, choking on her own tears. Sharon stared at her friend in shock, not quite expecting this sudden outburst.

"Andrea what is wrong sister?" Sharon asked as she led her to the den to sit down on the couch. They sat down on the couch and Sharon put her arm around Andrea trying to comfort her. "Andrea, please tell me what's wrong."

Andrea tried to compose herself enough to tell her story. As she slowly gained some control of herself she began to talk to her friend.

"Sharon, Mitchell cheated on me while we were in Biloxi."

"Oh Andrea, girl I am so sorry." Sharon wasn't sure just what to say. She wanted to be really careful about what she did say because she could tell her friend was taking this all very hard. Although Sharon had been down this road not long ago she didn't want to contaminate Andrea's thinking. They had always had different opinions on what happens after you discover your man has cheated and although Sharon was sincerely here for her friend she wondered if Andrea's opinion would change now that the shoe was on the other foot. Sharon said nothing more, waiting for Andrea to continue.

"He cheated with Monica. They spent the weekend together in this damn house while we were in Biloxi!" Andrea's whimper quickly turned into a shout.

"That bastard...!" Sharon hissed, not able to contain her anger. "Are you sure Andrea?"

"Yes I am sure."

"How do you know?" Sharon could not believe what she was hearing.

"He's in jail Sharon, my dad pressed charges on him for statutory rape."

"You are lying!" Sharon got up off of the couch, took the bottle into the kitchen and opened up the bottle of Remy Cognac. She pulled two glasses out of the cabinet and poured. She turned her glass up, emptying it with a few swallows and then refilled it before returning to the den. Andrea was still seated in the same position. "Here drink this girl. I'm thinking you might need it."

"I'm thinking you're right. I've been drinking since this morning and can't seem to get drunk, even a little bit. "

"Andrea, have you talked to Mitchell or Monica?"

"I went to the jail to see Mitchell and he would not talk girl. He acted as though the cat got his fucking tongue. He just sat there and stared. The bastard had the nerve to say it wasn't the time to talk about it!"

Indiscretions of a Married Man

"I know you are kidding."

"Sharon I wish to God I was, but I am not."

"Well what about Monica?"

"Can I tell you I had to beat that ass up in my parents' house?"

"Shut up! You're lying." Sharon said as she smiled at the thought of her whipping ass because that was so much not like her. Andrea began to laugh too, as she told Sharon how Monica was so remorseful in front of their parents but when she visited her room the next morning she was talking shit.

"No she wasn't talking shit." Sharon repeated as she poured them another round of Remy. She knew they were well on their way to being toasted but after a story like this they deserved it.

"Yeah, she said it wasn't her fault my husband couldn't keep his dick in his pants and that I shouldn't blame her. It's not her fault if I can't hold my man. Girl I blacked out and commenced to beating her young ass like she was a grown woman from off the streets."

They looked at each other and began to laugh at the thought of Andrea whipping up on Monica. The Remy had kicked in and they laughed for a while. As they continued to laugh sobs began to trickle through and tears streamed down both of their faces. Andrea cried, "I don't know what to do Sharon and it hurts so bad. The pain won't go away."

Indiscretions of a Married Man

"I know sister, I know. It's going to take time…a lot of time" Sharon cried for her friend and for the memory of herself in this very same situation with her husband years ago. It felt as though it happened just yesterday. Andrea and Sharon laughed a little and cried a lot throughout the evening. Eventually they passed out from cognac and emotional exhaustion.

The next morning Andrea and Sharon woke with slight hangovers. After showering they prepared a hearty breakfast. They sat at the table quietly eating, each in their own world, Andrea thinking of what her next step would be and Sharon thinking of what her next step was. "So what are you going to do about Mitchell?" Sharon asked between bites.

"I really don't know Sharon. I feel like I owe him a chance to explain himself before I make any drastic moves."

Sharon swallowed very hard trying to digest what her friend had just said. "You don't owe him a damn thing Andrea. The man fucked your sister and you owe him…"

"Yes I do, he is my husband."

"And because he is your husband that makes it okay? I don't think so."

Sharon took a deep breath trying not to let her past experience of infidelity with her husband take over her emotions. She really wanted Andrea to understand that her husband cheated and there was nothing right about that.

"We took vows Sharon and therefore I have to at least try."

"Try what? Please don't tell me that you are going to still be with him after he slept with your sister." Andrea could not believe what she was hearing come out of her friend's mouth.

"Sharon I know you don't understand but I have to try. He's my husband."

"Don't be so goddamn naive Andrea!! *YOUR HUSBAND* slept with your younger sister! What is left?"

"I don't know what is left. I just know I have to try." During Sharon's divorce they had several heated conversations about what happens after your spouse cheats. Although Sharon knew what stand Andrea took on the subject, she was so sure that being in this situation would have changed the way she felt about what one should do after they discover their spouse is cheating. She could not believe that her friend still felt the same way. Well she would have to just see for herself that nothing ever goes back to being the same.

Chapter 19

A week had passed since Andrea's visit to the jail, slowly panic began to seep in. Mitchell was sure by now someone had sat his wife down and told her the entire story. He sat in his cell wondering if he would hear from her again. He wondered who told her, what did they said to her and what did she think of him now.

Indiscretions of a Married Man

He went before the judge earlier in the week and his wife was not present. The judge advised him of his charges and that he definitely needed legal representation. He now knew that Andrea's parents had brought the charges against him. Although he wanted to blame someone he could blame no one but himself. It seemed as though his wife had abandoned him and help was not on the way. He had no property bond that was equivalent to $150 thousand dollars and he could not just sit in here and wait for a lawyer to fall from the sky. He needed to get out of this jail so that he could pull his life back together, what was left of it anyway. As Mitchell continued to sit in deep thought he realized at this point he would have to help himself and that no one was coming to his rescue. He sat contemplating the call that was inevitable...

After 24 hours of contemplating, Mitchell placed a call to his parents for help. His father answered the phone and Mitchell immediately began to explain. He told his father everything, not holding anything back and although his father could not believe his son's stupidity, he tried to understand his weakness. Robert Reid realized his son had gotten himself into a bad situation but no matter what, they would stand behind him. He assured his son that he would be in Atlanta on the next flight out. When the call ended Mitchell felt a great sense of relief that his father had not judged him. Once Robert Reid hung up the phone with his son he immediately called his attorney who assured him that he would

Indiscretions of a Married Man

begin handling the case right away. It would probably take a day or two before Mitchell would be released.

Robert and his wife Lynn decided they would check into a hotel after their visit with Mitchell, they had gotten in late and hoped they would still be allowed to visit with their son. As they stood in the lobby waiting to be cleared for their visit, both were deep in thought. They were not sure how they were going to handle this entire situation. They were both very sure that it would get worse before getting better. They were jolted from their thoughts as they heard their names called. They were directed to a small room where glass separated visitor from inmate. They sat and waited for their son to appear. After what seemed like forever Mitchell appeared on the other side of the glass. Robert grabbed his wife's hand, knowing this was too much for her. His wife always put on a façade to be strong for everyone else, when it was her who needed someone to be her strength at times. She was always strong for everyone else and Robert had come to really love that quality about her.

Mitchell sat quietly across from his parents. He felt relieved to see his parents on the other side of that glass. Just their presence made him feel as though everything was going to be all right.

"Hey mom, I am so sorry you had to come under these circumstances."

"Don't worry about that right now, baby. We need to concentrate on getting you out of this place," Lynn said as she slowly glanced at their surroundings. Looking past Mitchell you could see the other inmates watching television, using the phone, and just hanging out. Not a very nice sight, Lynn thought to herself.

"Mitchell, we've contacted Ray and he is working on getting you out as we speak. He said it might take up to 48 hours. But we won't leave until we have you out of here and this mess is cleared up." Ray was their family attorney as well as a good friend to Mitchell's father Robert. Tears formed in Mitchell's eyes and he wasn't really sure if they were tears of relief, joy, or sorrow. After a moment of thought he realized they were tears of relief because his parents were here, tears of joy to know that he was getting out of this hell hole and tears of sorrow because of what this mess had cost him. The sorrow overwhelmed all of the other emotions. Robert and Lynn watched as their son wept, giving him the time he needed to come to terms with the situation he had put himself in.

"I am so sorry," Mitchell said between sobs. "It's just been so much," Mitchell confessed as he attempted to pull himself together. For a brief moment they sat in silence.

"Mitchell, son, you are going to have to tell Ray exactly how you ended up in here. The charges against you are very serious and if you are found guilty you could go to jail and have to register as a sex offender. Your hearing is scheduled for next month and that is not too far away, we have got to be ready. Have you spoken to Andrea yet?"

Indiscretions of a Married Man

"No Dad. She hasn't returned since her first visit. It's been about a week, I guess she can't stand the sight of me right now…I really don't blame her," Mitchell said humbling himself.

"Don't wallow in your pity Mitchell. Hold your head up. You have to take responsibility for what you have created. You should not be proud of what you have done but be a man about it," Lynn said to her son.

As they sat for 45 minutes Robert and Mitchell discussed what happened and what they needed to do, Lynn drifted into her own thoughts. She heard from Robert what their son had done to land himself in this jail and she was not accepting of it. She was a woman first and although he was her son, she felt that he deserved just what his ass got. Maybe he'd think twice before he stepped outside of his next marriage. He didn't even have enough sense to take it away from home. Now look at the mess he had put everyone in. She could not feel sorry for him but he was her son. She knew this was not the place to tell him how she really felt but as soon as they got his ass out of this mess she was going to let him know a few things.

"Lynn…" Robert had called her name for the second time.

"Yes honey." She snapped out of her thoughts.

"The guard has signaled for us to leave." They rose from their seats to depart the area. Robert touched the glass in attempt to touch his son's hand. "It's going to be alright son. Hang in there. We're going to try to have you out by tomorrow. Stay strong."

Indiscretions of a Married Man

"Thanks Dad, love you, love you mom."

"I love you son. Don't worry we're here," Lynn said as they prepared to leave. They exited the room and continued their exit from the jail in silence; each absorbed in what they were up against. Not quite ready to confront the Brown family with this mess, they decided to check into their hotel and get some rest.

Robert and Lynn were awakened from the ringing of his cell phone. It was already daybreak and it seemed as though they had just laid their heads down to rest. Robert located his cell phone and answered. "This is Robert speak on it." As Lynn listened to her husband she thought how much she hated they way he answered his phone, thanking God he rarely answered their phone at home. His conversation was brief. It looked as though he exhaled deeply before hanging up the phone.

'Well Baby I hope you're ready for this day cause it looks like it's going to be a long one."

"It can't be any longer than yesterday I'm sure."

"Well we'll just see about that. That was Ray, he said we should be able to pick Mitchell up in another hour, he's being processed out."

"That's one part of the problem resolved."

"I have a feeling this problem has only began. I can't imagine what was on that boy's mind, Lynn."

"Oh yes you can Robert. SEX...!" Mitchell knows better. I can't believe him. I would like to string his ass up and beat the hell out of him for being so stupid."

"Lynn he's already suffering. I don't think you have to do much more to punish him. He's probably lost his wife, his home, and his respect. He really doesn't need your shit too. So please for now, keep it to yourself."

"I know baby, you're probably right. It's just that he has made me so damn mad."

"Just remember he is a grown man and he has to bear his own cross."

"Well what do you say to a little breakfast before we begin this journey?"

"Sounds like a winner."

Shortly after Robert and Lynn completed their breakfast at IHOP they went to the jail to pick their son up. Once they arrived at the jail there was a representative from Ray's law firm to meet them. He thoroughly explained all of the forms they were signing. Shortly after they completed the process with their signature of the property bond, Mitchell was guided through the lobby. Never had he felt better and never did he want to come back. A smile of relief stretched his face from ear to ear. He walked briskly toward his parents and embraced them tightly. "Thank you, mom and dad. Thank you so much."

"Don't thank us yet. It's far from over," Lynn said as she stared at her son.

"I still say thank you mom. I'm walking out of here thanks to you and dad."

"I'll go with that," Robert said as he squeezed his son's shoulder for assurance. Finalizing the bond, the Reid family thanked and exchanged handshakes with the Attorney. He then scheduled to meet with Mitchell two weeks from the date. They departed the jail and began to drive toward Mitchell's home. The closer they came to Mitchell's home the closer Mitchell came to the realization that the home he had would no longer exist.

CHAPTER 20

As they drove away from the jail Mitchell never looked back. The many things he had taken for granted a week ago he now appreciated. He sat in the back seat thankful for his parents. As they continued to ride, the streets and neighborhoods began to look familiar. The reality of where they were going slowly settled in. They were driving toward his house. Mitchell tried to put everything into perspective before he walked through his front door. He would have a lot of explaining to do and he wanted to be prepared. The ride from the jail was a quiet one. It seemed as though his parents

Indiscretions of a Married Man

were giving him time to be alone with his thoughts. As they pulled into his driveway Mitchell prepared himself for whatever he was about to walk into.

"Well Mitchell, I do believe this is your stop."

"Come on in and sit for a while."

"No son, I don't think that is a good idea. You have to work this out with your wife and I believe company is the last thing you need right now," said his dad.

"Call if you need us son and don't let things get out of hand." Mitchell listened to his parents without saying a word because he knew they were right.

As he got out of the car his parents assured him that they would see him tomorrow. He walked towards the front door, his body immediately tensed and his stomach knotted from the uncertainty of what was behind the door. He slowly walked towards the front door, turned the key and stepped inside. All was quiet. He expected the house to be in a total mess. It was apparent that Andrea wasn't home and he was relieved. "Thank God she's not home yet." As he walked through the house he looked for signs of what to expect when she returned. He walked up the steps to their bedroom. All looked normal until he opened the closet and saw none of his clothes. He began to check his chest of drawers, pulling out each drawer he saw that all of his belongings had been emptied from them as well. "What the hell did she do with my shit? I hope she didn't throw them away or there's going to be a problem." Then just as quickly he thought to himself, "I am tripping."

He exhaled as he went downstairs to check the garage for his car. It was not there, he assumed it was still parked at the job. He did notice quite a few boxes stacked against the wall. He walked closer to examine the boxes and realized they were filled with all of his belongings. Mitchell knew this meant his wife expected him to find a new address. "At least she put my shit in boxes and did not destroy them," Mitchell said aloud as he dug through the boxes in search of clean clothes to put on. Mitchell grabbed a white tank; gray sweatpants, underwear, socks and his sneakers then went back inside the house to shower. He took his time showering, enjoying the privacy of his home as he thought of the week he had to share a shower and toilet with more than a dozen strange men. After showering Mitchell dressed and went downstairs to the den. He stretched out on the black leather sofa and turned the television on not really interested in what was showing. He turned it on because he did not want to be alone with his thoughts. He eventually drifted off to sleep and the television watched him.

CHAPTER 21

Indiscretions of a Married Man

After a long night of talking and drinking with Sharon, Andrea felt she needed to go to the jail the next morning and hear what her husband had to say in his defense. She wanted him to explain what went wrong. She had so many questions she needed answers to. She refused to believe the story Monica had given her. There was no way that Mitchell would have willingly slept with her sister, Monica was a lying trick. She was no virgin and that was for damn sure. Andrea just never figured that her sister would go this low. She pulled into the parking lot of the jail and sat. She sat for fifteen minutes trying to rationalize why her husband slept with her younger sister. The longer she sat in the jeep the more convinced she was that she was not ready to see him and with that thought she pulled off. "What is wrong with me? Why can't I face my husband?" she asked herself aloud. Andrea was determined that she would not feel sorry for herself, as she drove towards home with tears flowing from her eyes. She pulled into her driveway attempting to wipe her eyes dry but the tears continued to flow. Mitchell heard her as she pulled into the driveway. "What the hell, I can't seem to stop crying," Andrea said as she reached the front door. Mitchell heard her before she came in. His heart beat as he watched the front door open and she step through it. She stepped inside and closed the door behind her. Kicking her shoes off at the door she decided to sit in the den for a while. As she walked towards the den her heart skipped a beat, noticing the television was on and Mitchell lying in front of it with his eyes fixed on her. "What in the hell was he doing here?" she asked herself. Andrea stood in the doorway of the den staring at her husband through tear-blurred eyes.

"Mitchell..." Andrea mouthed his name softly in barely a whisper. She was happy to see him but that instantly disappeared as the sight of him in the den jogged her memory.

"Hey baby...Andrea," Mitchell stumbled with his words and his stomach turned with nerves. He was so happy to see her and hear her voice. He had truly missed her but Mitchell knew it was time to put the truth on the table. There was no running from it now. He looked at his wife, her eyes full of pain and puffy from crying. He couldn't believe it was him who caused her pain. He had vowed never to hurt her and here they were because of his weakness and stupidity. He just wanted to fix it, make it the way it was but that seemed so long ago. In his heart he knew it would never be the same, he would give anything to take the pain he saw in his wife's eyes away.

"Why don't you come over here and sit down," Mitchell asked her as he got up from the sofa and walked towards her.

"What are you doing here?" Andrea asked her husband.

"I live here or has something changed."

"I meant, I thought you were still in jail, when did you get out?" Andrea continued to stand in the doorway refusing to take another step.

"This morning, my parents flew in last night."

Indiscretions of a Married Man

"Do they know what you did? Did you tell them about you and Monica?" Andrea's voice faded in and out. She watched his facial expression change instantly from slightly humble to overwhelming guilt.

"Yes I've told them what happened, Andrea," Mitchell said as he approached her.

"What did happen, Mitchell? Why would you do this to me?" Andrea cried. Mitchell took her into his arms, she tried to resist but was so emotionally exhausted she had no fight left in her.

"Come on baby," Mitchell said as he led her to the sofa in the den. Mitchell held Andrea tightly in his arms, rubbing and caressing her as she cried uncontrollably. Tears began to roll down his face as he whispered through her sobs, "I'm so sorry baby, I'm so sorry." Mitchell held Andrea close to him for what seemed to be an eternity as they cried together. After the tears, there was silence for a period of time before Andrea pulled from Mitchell's comforting embrace. Although she loved him more than anything in life she could not be weak for this man. She wasn't sure of how she would feel after hearing him out, the one thing she was sure of was that she had to hear from him what had happened between him and her sister that weekend.

"What happened, Mitchell?"

Mitchell took a deep breath and began to explain his wrong away. "Baby there is no way for me to make right what I have done and if I could erase this entire mess I would but…"

Indiscretions of a Married Man

"Just tell me what happened Mitchell, tell me!"

"Andrea let me finish, I need to tell you my way please…I'm trying to tell you."

"No you are not! You are trying to explain why you did it! I want to know what happened and I want to know right now!"

"Please listen baby, just hear me out."

"Did you sleep with her?" Andrea demanded as her patience flew out the door. Mitchell put his head down and wiped his face dry as Andrea yelled in his face. "Did you fuck her Mitchell? Answer the damn question!" Andrea instantly became angry and she was no longer quite so understanding.

"Yes. Yes. I slept with her but baby please let me explain." Mitchell pleaded.

"What in the hell is there to explain about you sleeping with my sixteen year old sister?"

"Andrea we were having problems, we had not made love in weeks."

"…And that's a reason to fuck my sister." Andrea responded.

"No it's not," Mitchell said as he humbled himself. "I did not intentionally sleep with your sister, she seduced me! Why would you allow her to come over and spend the night if you were not going to be there?"

"Oh so now it's my fault?" Andrea thought for a minute trying to compare what Mitchell was saying to what Monica had

Indiscretions of a Married Man

already said. "She said she called you before she came over, and you said you were not going to be in."

"She never called me, I came home and she was in our damn bed! I asked her what was she doing here and she said you were okay with it. I told her to get her ass out of our bed and she gets out of the bed buck ass naked. She walks past me deliberately rubbing her naked body against me. I got weak baby, I just got weak." Mitchell's voice became barely a whisper. "That was my stupidity, my stupid ass mistake."

Mitchell answered every question Andrea asked of him as honestly as he could. Andrea listened to him, staring him in the face to see if his eyes revealed any evidence of a lie. All she saw was a reflection of the pain she felt. Mitchell apologized over and over again. Tears ran freely down his face, he had put down his pride realizing his wife and marriage would never be the same again. Andrea reached out to comfort him. "He is my husband, we made a vow for better or worse," she repeated to herself. Although he was wrong she couldn't bear to see him in this state. Andrea placed her arm around her husband's shoulders pulling him close. He laid his head on her breast in an attempt of pulling himself together. Andrea wanted to comfort him as he had done her minutes ago. She rubbed his back and caressed his hair. Mitchell wrapped his arms around her waist stroking her back, "Baby I'm so sorry." Mitchell said, as he looked her in her eyes.

Indiscretions of a Married Man

"I know, Mitchell." Andrea whispered as she lightly kissed his face. Mitchell's mouth found Andrea's mouth. His probing tongue gently parted her lips. They embraced in long passionate kissing. Both missing what the other had to give, missing each other's love. Mitchell eased out of Andrea's embrace, lifted her from the couch and carried her up the stairs. He placed her on their bed and lay beside her, caressing and stroking every part of her body. Slowly their clothes came off and they lay naked fondling each other. Mitchell kissed Andrea's open mouth tenderly. He kissed her neck and then slowly moved his mouth to her breast, taking each nipple in his mouth. Mitchell parted her legs and his mouth traveled over her stomach and continued to travel until his tongue was between her thighs. He buried his face, Andrea softy moaned as her husband made love to her body with his mouth.

As she lay in bed naked with her husband's face buried between the thighs she closed her eyes and the image of her husband and her sister entwined together pierced through her thoughts. Her body tensed as she tried to force the image from her memory. Mitchell felt her tense but he assumed it was from the pleasure he was giving her and intensified the oral pleasure bringing her to a climax. He slid his body up next to his wife satisfied that he had satisfied her. For tonight that was more than enough, that satisfied him. He lay next to Andrea thanking God the worst was over and they could now begin to heal together, with that thought Mitchell dozed off to sleep. Andrea lay next to him thinking about the intense

Indiscretions of a Married Man

oral pleasure he had just given her. She wondered did he perform oral sex on her sister. She wondered how many times they had sex. She wondered if her sister fucked him better than she did. She wondered herself off into a deep sleep.

CHAPTER 22

Andrea woke up before Mitchell; she lay still in their bed as she remembered their night. As she thought of the conversation she would have with him this morning, it saddened her. She felt she needed time to think a few things through and she could not do that with Mitchell here. She eased out of the bed and showered in the guest room not wanting to wake him too soon at least until she figured out exactly what she would say to him.

Mitchell woke shortly after Andrea stepped into the shower. He lay in bed with a feeling of relief. It hadn't turned out as bad as he thought. He was surprised his wife let him make love to her after all that had happened in the past two weeks. He was grateful that she was willing to give him a chance and not beat him down about it. He got out of the bed to shower and thought to himself, "She will never have to worry about me again I will jack off before I even think about some new pussy. This was just a little too close for comfort. I almost lost everything behind pussy…never again!"

Indiscretions of a Married Man

Mitchell got out of the shower to dry off; Andrea was already dressed and looking out of the window. "Hey baby, care to share, I thought we could start our day with a little breakfast in bed…my treat," Mitchell smiled at his wife. Andrea forced a small smile to her face. Not quite sure how to tell her husband what she had thought about last night and all of this morning.

"What do you say baby, you feel like being my breakfast? I sure am hungry," Mitchell said as he licked his lips and smiled.

"Mitchell, ugh, I think we need to talk," Andrea said as she stumbled over her words. Please sit down I have something I need to say."

"What is it Andrea?" Mitchell asked, worried of what would come out of his wife's mouth.

"Last night. I think we both needed last night." Andrea was not sure how to say what she needed to say without crushing his feeling. She could tell from his earlier expression that he thought the worst between them was over.

"Baby I missed you so much. All I want to do is spend the rest of my life making up to you. I need you Andrea, not just last night but for the rest of my life."

He was making it very hard for her to say what she needed to say. "Mitchell, I need time."

"You need time for what Andrea?"

"I need time to sort this mess out and heal."

Indiscretions of a Married Man

"Okay baby I can understand that. I don't expect this to just go away over night and we pick up where we left off before all this mess happened. We both need time."

"Mitchell, I mean time away from you," Andrea instantly saw the joy turn to pain.

"Andrea baby we can get through this, we don't have to be apart, that's not going to help anything."

"It will help me Mitchell, I need room to think. I can't think with you here trying to apologize in everything you do."

"What do you want me to do Andrea? What are you telling me?"

"I think it's best for you to move out for a while."

"Move out! Where am I supposed to go Andrea? Why can't we work it out here together? What happen to for better or worse?"

"Mitchell I have not forgotten the vows we have taken. But those vows also included faithfulness! So please just understand I need time."

"What about last night Andrea?"

"We both needed last night Mitchell, but last night was last night. Just because we made love doesn't make it alright."

"It does for me."

"Not for me Mitchell. Last night while we were making love you want to know what I thought about? You and Monica! Did you make love to her the way you did me last night? Is she better than me in bed?"

"Baby, don't be ridiculous. It was a stupid ass mistake and I am sorry but we do not have to separate to fix it."

"You may not, but I do. Please don't make this any harder than it already is."

"It doesn't seem to be so hard for you!" Mitchell lashed out and then quickly apologized. "I'm sorry that wasn't necessary. So what do you want?"

"I want you to move out for a while."

"What is a while, Andrea?"

"I don't know. I just need some time."

"Okay fine. I'll try to be out before the end of this week."

"Thank you."

"No problem. If that's what you need to heal, who am I to resist?"

Andrea walked out of the room, down the stairs and out the front door. She got in her jeep and sat for a minute hoping she was doing the right thing. Mitchell stood in the middle of the room trying to figure out what just happened. He woke up thinking everything was going to be okay and now he was standing in the middle of the room trying to figure out where he would live.

CHAPTER 23

Indiscretions of a Married Man

Mitchell's worst fear had shown its face. He thought they'd be able to work this out under the same roof but apparently Andrea didn't feel the same way. Mitchell sat back on the sofa and began to replay their conversation in his mind. He began to think that this might be the beginning of the end to his marriage. They had shared tears of compassion and made passionate love the night before, he wasn't sure what had happened since then. He needed to talk to someone because this wasn't making a lot of sense to him right now. He picked up the phone and began to dial Darien's phone number. Darien and Mitchell had been friends since college. They both kept such a busy schedule that it was hard to visit one another as often as they should have but they tried to call each other regularly. Mitchell knew that whenever he needed a strong ear Darien was always there to listen and give him the best advice he could. He never judged him but he made him accountable for his screw-ups. He was the brother Mitchell never had and Mitchell needed some brotherly advice right now.

As the phone rang in Mitchell's ear he hoped that Darien was home. He had tried to reach him on his cell but that phone just rang and Darien never answered it. Just as he was about to hang up he heard Darien's voice, "Mitch, what's going on my brother?"

"Caller ID, huh."

"It helps man. It's been a while what's up? How have you been?"

"Has it been that long man?"

Indiscretions of a Married Man

"Seems like it brother but I always say no new is good news."

"Not always man not always…" Mitchell said humbling his voice.

"Are you alright?"

"What's your day looking like man? I need to borrow your ear."

"Always got time for you man. What do you say we meet me in about an hour at Dugan's on Memorial drive?" Darien said a little worried about his friend.

"Why don't I pick up something to drink and shoot out your way?" Mitchell said as the thought of being out right now was not appealing to him.

"That's cool too. I just thought you wanted to be out."

"No not today man." Mitchell said.

"Alright then I'll see you in about an hour."

"Yeah, an hour is good." Mitchell said as he thought about how he was going to get his car. "Well I guess I'll call pops." Mitchell dialed his father's cell phone. His father picked up on the first ring. "Hello."

"Hey dad what's going on?"

"I should be asking you that son. Are you okay?"

"Yeah, I'm okay, I need to pick up my car from my job can you give me a ride?"

"Sure I'll be there in fifteen minutes."

Indiscretions of a Married Man

Mitchell paced around downstairs while waiting for his father to arrive. He looked over all the pictures on the mantel of him and Andrea remembering the better times. He wondered would they ever be the same and although in his heart he knew the answer to that he wasn't ready to face it. He thought about his job. He had been there for seven years. He really enjoyed what he did but he wasn't sure he could face them after being escorted out by two detectives in the middle of the day. He thought about taking a little time off and trying something different. As he continued to think of where he would go from here he heard the horn blow. He grabbed his jacket and looked around once again before going through the front door. He locked the door and tried to put on his "Everything is fine" face and got in the car, "Hey dad."

"What's going on Mitchell? Is everything alright?"

"Yeah, everything is good."

"Did you get everything worked out with Andrea?"

"I did. We have both agreed that we need a little time apart to work through this."

"Are you sure you want to do that?" His dad asked looking a little confused.

"Yeah dad we talked about it this morning and we both think it's for the best right now."

"Well only you two know what's best for you."

"Yeah, where's mom?"

Indiscretions of a Married Man

"She was on her way down to the workout room. The hotel has a sauna and work out room downstairs. She didn't feel like riding and I didn't feel like working out."

"I heard that."

"So I guess you'll be the one moving out?"

"Most likely, isn't that the way it always goes."?

"Yes but can Andrea afford to keep the house if you two don't work it out."

"I doubt it dad. I guess she'll have to figure that one out." Mitchell quickly changed the subject to things going on back home. They talked about that for the remainder of the ride. Once they reached Mitchell's car, he was relieved. He didn't feel like talking to his dad about his marriage today. His father always had the practical answers but right now Mitchell did not want to hear practical. He wanted to swear a little bit and talk shit about how he had gotten himself into this situation in the first place and he just could not do that with his father. His father pulled up besides Mitchell's car and parked. "Have you contacted your job since you've gotten out?"

"When I got home I called in for a week out. I need a couple of days before I deal with them."

"Well Ray's office should be contacting you within the next week with a date for your preliminary hearing. You should try to get in touch with him this week so that you can go over what happened before the hearing."

"I will dad, just not today. I need a little time."

Indiscretions of a Married Man

"I understand son. Do you want to come back home for a while?"

"No dad. I'm okay."

"Your mother and I are going to pull out in a day or two. We were going to try and see Andrea's parents before we left."

"Good luck with that." Mitchell said.

"Well Mitchell it's only right that we try before we leave. We'll probably try to do that today. How's Andrea?"

"She is alright considering the circumstances." Mitchell was ready to wrap this conversation up. "Okay dad I will give you a call later. You and mom are leaving out in two days?"

"Yes. We've done what we came here to do. The rest is on you."

"Alright, I appreciate you, dad."

"I know son. I know." Robert watched his son as he got out of his car and into his own. He knew there was nothing he could do to ease his son's pain. Mitchell had sacrificed everything for a moment of weakness and Robert wanted to understand but he found it very hard to. He wondered what was going through his son's head when he did this. This was a lesson his son would learn alone, one that could change his marriage forever. He just hoped that his son realized what his moment of weakness had really cost him and everyone involved. With that thought he began to drive back to the hotel.

Indiscretions of a Married Man

As Mitchell pulled into the driveway Darien stepped out of his front door happy to see his friend. Darien stood 6'2 with skin that was the color of coffee beans. He had his hair evenly cut close to his head, brown eyes and a pretty smile to match. His body represented Gold's gym. "You're looking good man. Still working out huh?"

"I try my best. What's going on partner?"

"You wouldn't believe it if I told you. I picked up some Crown, is that okay?"

"That's cool," Darien said as Mitchell approached him. They embraced each other with a brotherly hug as they went inside the house. They went straight to the kitchen, pulled out two glasses and went to the den. They sat down and poured their first round of Crown. Mitchell looked around admiring how well Darien had decorated his house. "You still haven't found a woman to put in this house?"

"No and I'm not looking. I got too much going on right now."

"I hear you."

"What's up with you though? I know you got something you want to get off your chest. It's not every day that I am honored with your presence."

"Ah you know it's not like that. Man you would not believe the shit that I put myself into."

"What did you do Mitchell?"

Indiscretions of a Married Man

"I fucked around and slept with Monica, Andrea's sister." Mitchell said figuring just put it out there because there was no pretty way to say it.

Darien looked at Mitchell waiting for him to say he was kidding or something like that but he didn't. "Mitchell man, no you didn't."

"Yeah, I did." Mitchell confessed.

"How old is that damn girl… she can't be no more than fifteen years old." Darien asked as he became a little disappointed in his friend.

"She's sixteen, man."

"What in the hell were you thinking? Do you know how much trouble that will get you?" Darien could not believe his friend stepped over the line like that. Although he totally disapproved, he would not judge him because that was his friend and he loved him as a brother. He was not there to judge, just listen.

"Man, I came home and she was in my bed naked." They both turned their glasses up and then refilled before Mitchell continued.

"Where was Andrea?" Darien asked.

"She went to Biloxi with Sharon and Dee. I came home and Monica was in my bed. At first I thought she was Andrea…"

"Come on man!" Darien said not believing that at all.

"Serious. Andrea and I argued about her going and I thought she had come to her damn senses, changed her mind and decided to stay." Mitchell said as he tried to convince his friend.

Indiscretions of a Married Man

"When did you realize it was Monica?"

"When I turned on the light, then I asked her to get out of the bed and she jumps from beneath the sheets buck ass naked."

"But she's only sixteen, man." Darien said as he wondered what his friend could have been thinking.

"I know. I know. But that was the farthest thing from my mine when she was standing in front of me naked with a damn body like a grown woman."

"But she's not." Darien said as his disappointment in his friend increased.

Mitchell heard Darien but would not acknowledge his comment. "She brushed her body against me man and I just went weak."

Darien looked at his friend trying to see if he was serious. He wasn't sure if Mitchell realized what he had done.

"Andrea wasn't giving up shit and I was horny. I lost it. I fucked her man. I won't make an excuse for it. The bottom line is I was weak and I fucked her and now I am paying for the shit." Mitchell emptied his glass again and Darien refilled it. They were beginning to feel good. The alcohol seemed to loosen Mitchell up as he continued with his story. "I fucked her all weekend and reality didn't set in until it was time for Andrea to come home."

"Does Andrea know?"

"Oh she knows. Her parents had me locked up for statutory rape. I just got out of jail yesterday."

"Shit, man when did all of this happen?" Darien asked.

Indiscretions of a Married Man

"About two weeks ago." Mitchell said.

"Have you and Andrea talked about it?" Darien asked.

"Last night we talked about it and I made love to her. This morning she wakes up and tells me she needs time and that I need to move out for a while."

"Damn. Mitchell, I'm sorry. I know how much you love her."

"Yeah," Mitchell was quiet for a minute before continuing. "I guess I made my bed and now my ass will have to sleep in it." Half of the bottle was gone and it had begun to influence their thinking. They were feeling pretty good.

"That's a hell of a bed you made for yourself just for a piece of ass…" Darien said as they finished off their drinks.

"Yeah and I am sure that I am not finished paying for it!" Mitchell said as they laughed and joked for a while before they became quiet. They stared out of the window and sipped their drinks as each was caught up in the reality of Mitchell's situation.

"So have you thought about what you're going to do?" Darien asked Mitchell seriously.

"You know, I haven't really had time to think that far ahead. Everything is hitting so quickly. I told her I'd try to be out of there in about a week."

"Look I've got all this space up in here. Why don't you come on in out the rain and get your head together. I could use a little company and help on some of these bills." Darien hoped Mitchell would take him up on his offer because although they sat and joked about Mitchell's situation, he looked like his whole world had just been snatched from him.

"Thanks man, I really didn't know where I was going to go. She caught me off guard. She wants me out. She's packed all my shit in boxes and put them in the garage." Mitchell said with his head in his hands.

"Is she home now?" Darien asked.

"No she said what she had to say and left."

"Well you want to go and get your things now. You know my truck is outside."

"Maybe I should wait until she gets back." Mitchell said, still trying to hold on to the hope that she would change her mind.

"Wait for what Mitchell? She asked you to leave, she's packed your shit up, don't make it any harder on yourself than it already is man." Darien said.

"I guess you're right."

"I am. So sober your ass up and let's do this man!' They sat quietly for a few minutes. Mitchell knew that his friend was right, why procrastinate. She said she needed time so now she can have it. Mitchell began to feel a little better. He was glad that he decided to call Darien. "Yeah man you're right. You are so right. The more he thought about what Darien had said the more he was convinced Darien was absolutely right. "I'm ready." They headed out the door to the truck.

Indiscretions of a Married Man

They arrived at Mitchell's house thirty minutes later. Andrea's jeep was not there. She had not returned yet. Mitchell opened the garage and they began to load his boxes on the back of the truck. It took no time at all. "You ready to pull out man? Have you got everything?" Darien asked. Mitchell started toward the garage door that led to the house and paused. He decided that anything left behind would stay there because he really wasn't sure he could go into the house at this time without emotionally letting go. He had held on for most of the afternoon and he wanted it to stay that way. "Yeah man, I've got everything I need." They got in the truck and backed out, closing the garage door behind them. They drove in silence for what seemed like two miles before Darien broke the silence. "You okay Partner?"

"Yeah man I'm cool. I'll tell you the farther that house gets behind me the better my ass is feeling." They laughed together although they both knew there was not much funny at this point. "Now let's get back to the house and finish off that fifth." Darien said.

After they reached Darien's house they unloaded the truck placing the boxes in the den. They sat down to rest and Darien said a lot of things that helped Mitchell put his situation into perspective. He refused to feel sorry for himself. He decided to stay at his job and to report for work in the morning. He'd had enough time out. It was time to join society again. That would keep his mind occupied with more than just the thought of Andrea. Mitchell and Darien drank, talked and laughed well into the evening before deciding to retire to their own private space. "Hey Darien…" Mitchell called as he walked down the hall past Darien's room.

"What's that man?"

"Thanks, thanks a lot."

"No problem."

Mitchell began to move the boxes from the den to the room that was to be his new home.

Chapter 24

After pulling out of the driveway Andrea decided to shop a little and treat herself to lunch and some quality time alone. She needed the time alone to clear her thoughts. Although she wasn't sure she wanted Mitchell to move out she knew it was what she was supposed to do. Mitchell said he would try to be out by the end of the week. She didn't think it would be so soon but maybe it was for the best. She was sure Mitchell would help for a while but she knew she could not afford the house. "I'm thinking too far ahead, he hasn't even moved yet," she told herself. Andrea finished up her lunch, moved to a table outside and she then ordered a glass of Chardonnay. She sipped her wine as she observed the different things going on outside of the restaurant and tripped on what she was observing. She tried not to think about the condition her marriage

Indiscretions of a Married Man

was in. By her third glass of Chardonnay Andrea was feeling quite tipsy and could think of anything but her husband and her marriage. The wine had intensified her thinking and she began to question herself. She questioned if she would be able to make peace with her sister, if she would be able to love and trust her husband as she did before this all happened and most of all if she would be able to stand by her vows "for better or worse." She spent the remainder of the afternoon visiting with Sharon who didn't live far from the restaurant. She was in no great condition to drive too far. Andrea relaxed and spent most of the evening at Sharon's. As she prepared to go home, she was sure Mitchell would be waiting for her to come through the door. He would probably try to talk her into changing her mine and they would probably end up in bed. Although not a bad idea, she wasn't so sure that was what she needed right now.

Driving towards home she thought about the conversation between herself and Sharon. When she told Sharon that she asked Mitchell to move out and she was surprised at Sharon's respond. *"Why would you put him out if you plan on remaining married to him? If you were divorcing him that would be another thing but your intention is to try and make it work. At least that's what you said, Right? Sharon asked.*

"I need time to think this through." Andrea said.

"Well, you're feeding him to the wolves by asking him to move out. It seems to me that if he were there every day trying to

show you that he's sorry, you could determine whether he was sincere or not."

"You have a point. I didn't even think about it like that. I guess that would just make it worse than it is." Andrea said.

"He doesn't have to be gone for you'll to work through it." Sharon tried to convince her friend.

"I guess you're right." Andrea agreed.

Sharon had really surprised her. Andrea thought she would be cheering about Mitchell moving out. Now she wasn't sure that was what she really wanted. She really valued Sharon's opinion and advice. Maybe she was being too hasty in asking him to move out. The closer she came to their house the closer she came to changing her mine.

She pulled into her driveway and noticed that the house was completely dark. It was only nine o'clock she thought to herself, too early for Mitchell to be sleeping. She used the garage opener and began pulling her jeep inside of the garage. As she pulled into the garage she noticed the boxes that she had packed all of Mitchell's belongings in were gone. No trace that they had ever been there. Her heart skipped a beat at the thought of Mitchell being gone. She got out of the Jeep in a hurry and went into the house calling out Mitchell's name, no answer. She thought maybe he had unpacked the boxes and she then turned lights on throughout the house looking in every room, in his closet, and in his chest of drawers. No sign of her husband, Mitchell was gone. She sat down on the couch and stared at the walls. She looked towards the phone as if that would make it ring and noticed the message light was blinking. There was a message on the phone. She hoped it was Mitchell calling to say he was on his way back home. She nervously checked the messages. There were three. The first was her father asking her to call as soon as she got in. She had not been over there since she whipped Monica's ass and had not planned on going over there as long as she was there. The second message was from Mitchell. She slowly sat down on the couch not sure of what her husband's message would say. As she listened she heard Mitchell's voice. *"Andrea I've decided to move out this afternoon to make it easier for us both. You said you needed time and I can only give you that. You know that I love you very much and I am sorry baby. I am really sorry for fucking up. I will give you a call when I get my head together. This isn't easy for me. It's the hardest thing I've ever had to do. I love you. I'll call soon."* Andrea continued to hold the phone to her ear as tears rolled out of her eyes with the realization that he was gone. She had gotten home too late. She didn't even know where he was and didn't want to start calling his cell since he had not bothered to call hers when he was moving out. "He's gone, he's really gone."

Chapter 25

Indiscretions of a Married Man

After moving out of the house I returned back to work. The hardest part of that was walking through that front door was knowing that everyone remembered me being escorted out by two detectives and me wondering who actually knew what happened that day. I guess that was my own paranoia because the day went smooth, everyone welcomed me back like I had been gone for a long time when it had actually been about two weeks. I had been staying late at work to try and catch up over two weeks of work that was patiently waiting my return.

"Mr. Reid, it is five fifteen and I am out." Tonya buzzed through the intercom. She's running a little late today. Every day since I have been back at the office Tonya will buzz me to let me know it is five o'clock, time to pack up and go home. Although she gets out of here on time, I never make it. Overtime has become therapy for me.

"Thanks Tonya. You're getting out of here?"

"Yes I am. I'm about to forward the phones to the answering service because everyone has left for the day except you again."

"Is there any way my line can ring directly to me while I am here. I am expecting a call from Darien shortly."

"Yes I can do that. Is there anything you need before I take off for the day?"

"No Tonya, that is it have a good evening and I'll see you in the morning."

"Okay. Don't work too late Mr. Reid."

Indiscretions of a Married Man

"Never…"

Mitchell got up from his desk and came out of his office to make sure everyone had left for the day because he did not want any surprises. Once he was sure everyone was gone he could leave his office door open and still have the quiet he needed to concentrate on getting his work complete. He returned back to his office and turned on the radio he kept on his desk. 87.7 was his station of choice because it was strictly about grown folk's music and old school which was enough to allow his mine not to wonder. He began to work away the remainder of the work pile. Mitchell was so caught up in the good sounds and his work that when the phone rang it startled him. "This has got to be Darien." Mitchell said as he picked up the phone. "GTB, Mitchell speaking."

"Darien, what's going on man?"

"Sounding mighty corporate there partner."

"A couple of us are heading to that jazz club on Roswell road, can't remember the name right now but come on and join us for a while."

"You mean TABU? What's going on there, man?"

"It's Wednesday Mitch, Ladies Night. It gets packed up in there man and they party hard for over the hump day."

"I don't know Dee I'm buried in work."

"Man it's been about three weeks and that's all your ass has been doing is working from 5am to 10pm. Breathe man, let that shit

Indiscretions of a Married Man

go! Come on out and have a good time. I'll swing through and pick you up if you don't want to drive."

"Alright Dee, Alright, what time are you talking about?"

"In the next hour…"

"Why so early, man?"

"Mitch, it is about to be 7:00."

"You're kidding?"

"Working too hard brother," Darien smiled. "Do you want me to pick you up?"

"No man. I'll just meet you there."

"We are about to leave. Don't bullshit me Mitchell. You're coming right?"

"Yeah man, I'm about to pack it up. I'll see you in an hour."

"Alright… Later."

"Later."

"I guess all work and no play can make a boring ass life." Mitchell said aloud after hanging the phone up. He had done nothing but work since moving in with Darien. Hoping that would keep him from thinking about anything other than work. As Mitchell began to organize his work for tomorrow the phone rang again. "Damn this must be Darien making sure I'm pulling out" Mitchell thought out loud. "GBS, Mitchell speaking."

"Hello…" spoke a soft voice in almost a whisper.

"Hello, this is Mitchell."

"Mitchell..." Mitchell's heart skipped a beat once he recognized the voice.

"Hey, it's me Andrea..."

"Hey..." He was not prepared for this. Mitchell had not spoken with Andrea since he and Dee moved the boxes out of the garage. He had not called her because he knew that talking to her and begging would only hinder him from focusing on getting his life back in order. What did she want? He was happy to hear from her but not ready for her to fuck his head up again. He wasn't over the last conversation they had.

"How are you?" Andrea asked.

"I'm doing the best that can be expected ...and yourself? How are you?"

"Okay I guess." Andrea replied.

"Look Andrea I haven't called because..." Mitchell said trying to offer an explanation.

"I know why you didn't call Mitchell. You left me a message explaining that after you moved out." Mitchell detected an immediate change in her voice but decided not to address it. He remained silent for a moment.

"Yeah, that's what you wanted... time. So that is what I gave you." Mitchell replied with slight attitude.

"Couldn't you have waited until I returned?" Andrea asked.

"Waited for what Andrea? Wait for you to return, so that I could beg you to stay."

Indiscretions of a Married Man

"No so that we could have talked before you left."

"There was nothing more to talk about. You said you wanted me out and I moved out." Mitchell said as he began to think that this woman had a lot of nerve.

"I never told you I wanted you out Mitchell."

"Well… time. To me it means the same thing, out!" Mitchell said wondering why she was calling after a damn month. He loved her so much and he waited everyday for three weeks for her to call and never one fucking time did she call. Now she calls… for what? Now he was angry.

"I need to talk to you Mitchell."

"Talk I'm listening." Mitchell began to feel some kind of way and it began to come out in his voice.

"Not over the phone. There are a few things we need to work out." This phone call was not going the way Andrea imagined it in her mine over and over again. She had picked up the phone so many times in the last three weeks to call Mitchell but she just didn't know what to say. She didn't know how to say please come home, let's work it out. She didn't know how to say you fucked up but we took vows and I love you enough to try. She didn't know how to put down her pride.

"Andrea I don't think it is a good idea for me to see you right now. I am not quite ready for that." Mitchell was trying to figure what it was that she wanted.

"Mitchell I need help. It's the first of the month and the bills are coming in."

"I know that Andrea. I am one step ahead of you. I get paid on the 15th and I had already planned on giving you some money. How much do you need?"

"I don't know. I just need help with the mortgage."

"I'll give you a call on the 15th."

"Okay. Thanks."

"Yeah…" There was silence for a brief moment.

"Mitchell, the real reason I called was to tell you that I love you, please let's work it out…" More silence. Andrea waited for a response but the only one she got was the dial tone. Mitchell had hung up the phone immediately after he said "yeah". Andrea held the phone in her hand for a brief moment. "I guess he really is adapting to that space I asked him for. Well maybe it's for the best that he didn't hear me." Andrea hung up the phone and returned to work. She had been moved to the evening shift at her request since she returned to work.

"I can't believe after a month the only thing that prompts her to call is because the bills are about to be due. I've been sitting my ass in this office, busting ass just to keep from calling her and asking to come home. What in the hell is wrong with me?" Mitchell had gotten so angry with himself for expecting something different from the call that he left the mess spread out on his desk, turned all lights out and headed towards the door on his way to TABU. Darien was right, why in the hell am I moping around waiting. Fuck that! No more. No more!"

Chapter 26

Mitchell pulled into the parking lot of the TABU club looking for a parking space. Darien was right it was pretty packed in here. He pulled in and let the staff outside park his car. He did not feel like the aggravation. It had been months since Mitchell had been out. Andrea never wanted to go out as a couple when they were together and he chose not to because he didn't want her to think it was okay for her to go without him, he enjoyed time with his wife at home. He got to the door and had to pay $15.00 to get in. "Damn Darien didn't tell me about the charge," he thought as he reached in his pocket for his wallet. As he was handing his money to the door Darien appeared from nowhere, "I got it man. Don't worry about it." Mitchell put his money back into his pocket and followed Darien.

"Damn man, when did cover charge get so expensive? $15.00! Does a damn free drink come with that shit?" Mitchell asked.

Indiscretions of a Married Man

"Sorry Mitch. We're at the table over in the corner. What you drinking?"

"I'll take a shot of crown. You were right about the women." Mitchell said as he took inventory of the room.

"Yeah, I told you so!" Darien said.

Mitchell and Darien found their way to the bar. As Darien ordered their drinks, Mitchell looked around in pleasure at the sight of all the beautiful women out tonight. "Enjoying the view I see," Darien said to Mitchell as he handed him his drink. It's cool. It's real cool." Mitchell said as they walked to the table.

"Hey, this is my boy Mitchell." Everyone at the table threw up a hand as if to say hello, it was a nice little crowd about five other brothers sat at the table. They all seemed to be enjoying the music and drinks. Their table was located by the dance floor towards the rear of the club; it was perfect seating for a perfect view of the ladies. Mitchell had forgotten how interesting the club scene could be at times. He sat back and relaxed with everyone else as the rounds kept coming. "You enjoying yourself man?" Darien asked.

"Definitely, I needed this. I had forgotten how to unwind."

"See there is life after marriage." Darien laughed.

"I guess so. Thanks for making me realize that." Mitchell replied.

"No problem. You heard from Andrea?"

"As a matter of a fact I have not heard from her since I moved in with you. But can I tell you she called me before I left the

Indiscretions of a Married Man

office to tell me she needed help with the bills!" Mitchell said getting pissed all over again at the thought.

"You're bullshitting me, right?" Darien said as he laughed.

"No sir. I am dead ass serious. Andrea called for money after three weeks of nothing...for money."

"Ain't that some shit?" Darien said.

"Yeah that's what I said." Mitchell replied.

"What'd you say to her?"

"I told her to hit me up on the 15th when I get paid. You know I don't mind giving a helping hand but I thought we were more than that man. You know?" Mitchell said.

"I hear you. Enough about her, you can't let her steal your joy man!"

"I know that's right!" Mitchell said as he turned his glass up and emptied it. "I think I'm going to step to the bar for another drink."

"You don't have to man, we've got a waitress." Darien said.

"I know but I'd like to mingle a little bit and really see what's happening in here." Mitchell said still angry about his earlier conversation with Andrea.

"Alright brother, do your thing." Darien smiled at the thought that his friend was beginning to loosen up and live a little.

Mitchell got up from his seat and began to wander through the crowd. He strolled to the bar and squeezed in to order his drink. "Fit right in why don't you." Mitchell found himself almost in the lap of a very attractive lady. Realizing he had pushed his way without considering the people sitting at the bar, embarrassment flooded his face. "I am so sorry. I didn't mean to…"

"It's okay. I was just messing with you." The young lady replied jokingly.

"Yeah but you were right, the least I can do is buy you a drink."

"I'll go for that." said the very attractive lady in her sexiest voice.

"What are you drinking?" Mitchell asked.

"A glass of Riesling wine would be nice."

"Coming right up," Mitchell said as he smiled at the lady. She was light complexioned with a very close curly boy cut. She wore very little makeup, "Natural beauty," Mitchell thought to himself. He ordered the drinks and began to walk away. "The least you could do is drink with me since you bullied your way in. My name is Tracy."

"Please to meet you Tracy. I'm Mitchell. I guess you're not going to let me live that down huh?"

"Not just yet." She smiled.

"God she is gorgeous." Mitchell continued to think as she smiled. They drank their drinks and talked enough to find out a little bit about each other. After they finished their drinks Mitchell offered her another that she declined due to the fact that it was getting late and she needed to call it a night. "I know what you mean.

Indiscretions of a Married Man

I have to get up pretty early myself. Can I offer to walk you to your car?"

"I would like that." Tracy said as she got up from her seat. Mitchell then escorted out of the club to her car.

"You must have gotten here a little late." Mitchell said.

"Oh you can tell from where I parked huh?" Tracy replied.

"Yeah… This place gets pretty packed I see."

"It does. You haven't been here before?" Tracy asked.

"Yes but it has been so long ago I don't remember it being like this, especially on a Wednesday night."

"It's like this every Wednesday because of ladies night." Tracy said.

"Do you come here often?" Mitchell asked.

"That depends on what you call often. I probably come three times a week."

"Well I'm glad I caught you out tonight." Mitchell smiled at his forwardness.

"I am too Mitchell." Tracy said as she pulled out her keys to unlock her car door. Mitchell politely removed the keys from her hand and unlocked her car door. He opened the door and stepped to the side so that she could get in and handed her the keys back. Once Tracy was in the car Mitchell closed the car door and prepared to say goodbye. He stood there wanting to ask for her number because he had really enjoyed her company this evening but he wasn't sure how to go about it. "Can I give you my phone number?" Tracy asked.

Indiscretions of a Married Man

Damn she must have been reading my thoughts. Mitchell smiled as he said, "I would like nothing more." Tracy wrote her number down on the back of a business card and handed it to Mitchell. "Good night Mitchell."

"Good night Tracy." As she drove off, Mitchell made his way back into the Jazz club to check on Darien and the rest of the crew. Once Mitchell got to the table he could see that they were preparing to leave. "Where'd you go to get that drink man?" Darien smiled.

Mitchell laughed, "To the bar."

"Well hell, where was the bar?" Darien joked.

"I mingled a little bit." Mitchell could not seem to wipe the smile from his face."

"Okay. Glad to see you haven't forgotten how." Darien smiled.

"Me too..."

"You ready to get out of here?"

"Yeah, I'm ready." Mitchell said.

Mitchell and Darien said good night to the rest of the crew and walked toward the exit. "You enjoy yourself tonight Mitch?"

"More than you can imagine." Mitchell smiled.

"I guess that has to do with your mingling, huh?"

"Yes indeed."

Indiscretions of a Married Man

Chapter 27

Andrea pulled into her driveway from work and thought of how empty she felt each time she entered the front door. Upon entering the house she went straight to the den, which was where she spent most of her time these days. That was where her computer was set up. Since Andrea had been working second shift she had no time for any social life. Dee had told her about POF, a social network, web sites that were supposed to be where you could meet people. Andrea registered with them and had been chatting with men from as far as New York and she loved it. It was quite entertaining for her because when she got off and everyone else was sleeping a conversation was only a keystroke away. Andrea never gave her name, on the social networks she was Chocolate that way she kept her true identity private, "You never know whom you could be talking with, better safe than sorry." Andrea thought aloud. After spending an hour on POF.com Andrea relaxed on the couch and began checking her home phone messages. She checked her messages faithfully hoping that a message from Mitchell would be there but once again nothing from him. There was a message from her father again. She had not returned any of their calls nor had she been over to visit with them like she did before this mess happened. She sat for a moment and stared at the phone before finally deciding to call her parents back. As Andrea listened to the phone ringing on

Indiscretions of a Married Man

the other end she wondered what her father wanted with her. "Hello…"

Andrea immediately recognized her younger sister's voice. Damn Monica would pick up the phone. "Hello," Monica said again.

"Let me speak to my father!" Monica quickly placed the phone on the table not wanting to say any more to her sister than she had to. Andrea could hear Monica calling for their father to come to the phone. "Hey there stranger," Her father said.

"Hey dad…"

"Why haven't you returned my calls baby?"

"Oh daddy, I've been so busy…" Andrea said.

"Come on now you can do better than that." Her father said.

"Okay dad. I'm sorry. How have you and mom been?"

"We are okay. We're more concerned about you. It's been over three weeks since we've heard from you, baby. What's going on? Are you okay?" Her dad asked.

"Yeah daddy, I told you that I am fine." Andrea replied.

"Have you spoken to Mitchell about this mess?"

"Yes I spoke with him." Andrea answered but really did not want to get into this conversation with her dad because she knew he was still salty about the situation.

"Has he told you that his preliminary hearing is this week?"

"No. He's not living here right now. I don't talk to him regularly."

Indiscretions of a Married Man

"Good for you baby, good for you." Her father praised her not knowing it was not her choice.

Andrea did not want to hear his praises to her for putting Mitchell out. What would he say if he knew it was not her final decision for him to move? She knew her father had not been crazy about Mitchell in the past but now she was sure he would not try to disguise it at all. "What were you saying about a hearing?" Andrea asked.

"He has a hearing next week, I believe it is Wednesday. I was calling to see if you had been notified."

"No I don't think they would notify me dad. I think they would contact Mitchell."

"Are you going to the hearing baby?"

"I doubt it. Unless I have to be there I choose not to go."

"Well your mother and I have to be there since we are the one who pressed the charges."

"What about Monica? She doesn't have to be there?"

"Yes she has to be there as well. Did you know that Mitchell's parents were here?"

"Yes they flew in to post bond for him." Andrea answered, wishing he would move on to a different subject but she knew that was not happening.

"Unbelievable. You know they came by here to talk with us about this mess. We tried to call you but as usual you did not answer the phone nor did you return the call." Her father said, trying to inform his daughter of all that was going on.

"Oh really and why did they come over here?"

"They came to offer their apology for their son's misbehavior. They are good people and they don't deserve to have a son like that. I feel sorry for them…"

"Okay dad I have to go now. I'll talk to you later." Andrea said knowing it was really time to go now. Even though she was not Mitchells fan right now she didn't want him bashed by anyone, including her father.

"Why don't you visit anymore baby?" he asked.

"I am not ready to see Monica dad. It has nothing to do with you and mom."

"Would it be okay if we drop in occasionally to check on you and make sure you're getting through this?"

"Sure." Andrea said and privately thought, I will make it my business to never be home until you can find something else besides Mitchell to talk about.

"We are not the enemy baby. We are here to help you all you have to do is call."

"Okay dad. I have to go. Bye."

"I love you". Her father said.

"Love you too." Andrea hung the phone up and thought about all her father had said. She had no way of getting in touch with Mitchell except for his work number. His cell phone was disconnected. She had not asked where he was staying and he had not volunteered the information. "I guess I'll just call his job tomorrow and find out whether or not I need to be at his hearing." Andrea said hoping this hearing did not require her presence.

Chapter 28

Mitchell sat at his desk feeling pretty damn good for a Monday morning. Since last Wednesday he had began to live a little outside of work. Darien had shown him quite a few spots over the weekend. Thursday after work they went to Jay's, the neighborhood bar, drank a few beers and shot a little pool, Friday night they went back to Taboo on Roswell road, Saturday they went out to Grant park to grill out with a few of Darien's partners. Sunday they went to Café 290 and listened to a little afternoon jazz. They retired early and woke up fresh on Monday to start a new week.

It had been a lovely weekend. Mitchell had not given Tracy a call yet, he just held on to the number. He realized it was too soon for him to try and get involved in any way with another woman, especially when he was still very much married and in love with his wife. He was beginning to enjoy his social life. He now understood why he was so possessive and jealous when it came to Andrea. It was because he had no business of his own, all he did was go to

Indiscretions of a Married Man

work, come home and wait for her to get there. "Damn, I didn't realize what I was missing. There is so much to do in Atlanta," he thought aloud knowing he had to give much thanks to his boy Darien for giving him a reality check.

The intercom buzzed in bringing Mitchell from his weekend back to the office. "Mr. Reid, call on line one."

"Thank you Tonya." Mitchell picked up the line. "Mitchell Reid speaking"

"Hey there Mitchell, this is Ray. How's it going?"

"I can't complain Ray. I am just taking it one day at a time."

"I was calling to remind you that your preliminary hearing is Wednesday. I need for you to come into my office before Wednesday so that I can go over a few things with you."

"I can do that today when I get off, if 5:30 is not too late."

"No that's fine. I'll see you then…"

"Ray, this preliminary hearing will I need to tell what happened again?"

"Mitchell my friend, you won't even have to be there I will handle it all. I'll explain when you get here this evening."

"Okay well that's good to hear. I'll see you this evening."

Mitchell sat for a minute and quietly thanked the Lord. Everything seemed to be coming together. He had not felt this good in a very long time, considering what he was going through he felt blessed. Mitchell knew that if his lawyer had notified him, the Brown family's attorney had notified them. That meant someone

Indiscretions of a Married Man

from the family had notified Andrea. He wondered would she contact him to give him words of support or something, hell just call because despite it all she still loved him. As fucked up as the situation was he was still her husband and he loved her very much. He made a mistake and was willing to spend the rest of his life making it up to her if she had allowed him. He wondered if she still cared, or had his actions killed that feeling for her. "Well I guess I will know where I stand with her by Wednesday," Mitchell said aloud. He got up from his desk, took a deep breath and decided it was time to take a smoke break, which was something he did not do often. He was a bit nervous about Wednesday but he felt like the Lord would take care of him. Upon returning from break Mitchell dug deep into his work until it was time to make his appointment with Ray.

Mitchell arrived at Ray's office thirty minutes early. He was kind of anxious to get this entire event behind him. Ray seemed to be prepared for him although he was very early. The administrative assistant showed Mitchell into Ray's office.

"Mitchell. Decided to come a little early I see." Ray said as he stood to shake Mitchell's hand.

"How's it going Ray? Not intentionally, I can wait outside if you're not ready for me."

"I'm always ready." Ray smiled as he shuffled through a desk full of papers. "Okay let's see if I can locate your file on this desk." Ray opened Mitchell's file and went over the statement that

Indiscretions of a Married Man

Mitchell had given him a few days after he was released from Dekalb County. Mitchell had given as accurate an account of what happened as he could. After going over Mitchell's story to ensure they had not missed anything Ray then proceeded to tell Mitchell what his investigation had turned up on his sweet innocent under aged sister in law. "First thing first, we had an examination done on Monica because her parents insisted that she was a virgin and you had taken advantage of her innocence. That examination has proven that not only was she not a virgin but she has been participating in sex for quite some time."

"I am not surprised and I don't understand how her parents could be so blinded." Mitchell said although he was very much surprised because he thought she was a virgin as well and she sure felt like it to his manhood. "Damn…" Mitchell whispered.

"We also had all medical records pulled on her and she has been treated in the past for a sexually transmitted disease at the clinic, which I am sure her parents have no knowledge of."

"You have got to be kidding. I can't believe she has gotten around like that." Mitchell said in a state of shock.

"That's not even the half of it. We contacted a woman who states she had to threaten Monica to keep her away from her husband. She is willing to come to the hearing and testify."

"How did you find out about her?" Mitchell asked stunned that he thought he had stolen her innocence.

Indiscretions of a Married Man

"We can't tell you everything Mitchell," Ray smiled." Mitchell continued to listen as Ray went on. Mitchell knew Monica was no angel but he had no idea she was tricking like that. He had not even used protection because he had assumed she was a virgin and here it was it sounded like she had more experience than him! What was he thinking? He could have caught something or worse scenario… pregnancy. Mitchell continued to think to himself and came to the conclusion that he really did not know what he was doing that weekend. He had really put himself out there for a piece of ass. "Never again…"

"Excuse me? Did you say something Mitchell?"

"No Ray I was just thinking aloud about how I allowed myself to get in this mess for a little sex."

"It does happen, Mitchell, so don't beat yourself up over it. It seems this young lady has more sexual experience under her belt than the average older woman. I don't think her parents are going to want this to go to trial, they can't win. There is no way the charge of statutory rape is going to stick once I expose all of this to the judge."

"What will happen then?"

"If they are smart they will settle at this hearing with a lesser charge. I'm sure they don't want their daughter's dirty laundry aired in court."

"If they decide to go with a lesser plea, what would the charge then be?"

Indiscretions of a Married Man

"It would probably be aggravated assault but it would still be a felony."

"You mean I will have a felony charge on my record behind this."

"Unfortunately yes you will and if they decide not to settle and their case is won you would have to register as a sex offender. That is what we are really trying to avoid aside from prison."

"I won't be on probation or anything like that will I?"

"We are going to try to avoid that as well but I can't promise you that Mitchell. You may have to do a couple of years of probation and pay a fine. But I am going to try my best."

"Thanks. This shit, ugh excuse me…" Mitchell said.

"That's okay I've heard it before and a little bit worse."

"I just can't believe this." said Mitchell.

"I hate to say it Mitchell but that's what happens when a minor is involved and sometimes it can get uglier than this. It's just your luck that this minor has a not so pretty past history and hopefully her parents won't want to pursue because of that. One way or the other we will know by this time Wednesday."

"And you said that I don't have to be there, correct?"

"That is correct unless you choose to be."

"No I'd rather not. I don't really feel like facing her parents. They already hated me I can only imagine how they feel about me now."

Indiscretions of a Married Man

"I understand completely. Well if you have no more questions, our business here is done."

"No sir, I have no more questions." Mitchell replied.

"I will contact you Wednesday as soon as I come out of court."

"What time is court?"

"It will be at 9:00 in the morning."

"Alright Ray thanks for everything."

"No problem."

Mitchell left Ray's office not knowing whether to feel positively or negatively charged. He decided that he would remain neutral until Wednesday was over and done with.

Chapter 29

Mitchell went to work the next morning with the intent of working the day away so that he could get through and past Wednesday morning. He worked straight through noon before the intercom interrupted his steady flow. "Mr. Reid you have a call on line two."

"Thank you Tonya. Who is it? Did they say?" Mitchell asked because he was awaiting Andrea's call. Tomorrow would be his hearing and he hoped that if she cared anything about him she would at least call.

Indiscretions of a Married Man

"No sir, Mr. Reid."

"Thank you. Mitchell Reid speaking..."

"Hey Mitch..."

"What's going on Darien?"

"Not much man. I know tomorrow is the big day and we've been kind of missing each other at the house. In the event that I don't see you before tomorrow morning I just wanted to say I hope everything goes okay man. Keep the faith, it'll work its way out."

"Darien, I appreciate that brother."

"Talk to you later, have to earn this paycheck." Darien said.

"Yeah I hear you. Later."

"Later."

Mitchell disconnected the call and sat for a minute appreciating the friendship that he had with Darien. He could not have asked for a better friend. When no one else was in his corner he could no doubt depend on Darien, no questions asked. "That's what I'm talking about, my brother!" Mitchell said aloud.

Andrea began her week in a computer training class that she registered for. Her job offered the class for free. The class began at 1:00 in the afternoon and ended at 8:00 in the evening. The class was scheduled to last one week. Their first break of the day was given at 4:00. She would use that break to call Mitchell. She was sure his hearing was tomorrow. Although she refused to be there she wanted to wish him the best. He had slept with her sister and she believed that he told her the truth about that night. She asked him

Indiscretions of a Married Man

quite a few questions and he honestly admitted that he had gotten weak. What he did was wrong but she tried to understand how it could have happened. She loved her husband and wanted to get through this so that they could try to get back to where they were. She just wasn't sure that would be such an easy task now that he was out of the house.

Mitchell watched the clock as the day ticked right away. He had completed the follow up calls to each of his clients, checked all of his email messages and responded to each one. He completed the contract he had been working on for the past six weeks and finalized the report. He also completed his agenda for Wednesday. He was not the one to shuffle papers to make his eight hour day. He glanced at the clock for a final time. He couldn't believe he had gotten so much accomplished by 3:15. "Not bad." Mitchell complimented himself. No reason to hang around here. That was one of the things he loved about his job, he was salaried and his hours were dictated by his workload. Whether he completed his workload in 4 hours or 10 hours he was able to end his day with the same pay. With a smile on his face Mitchell began to pack it up.

"Tonya I am gone for the day." Mitchell said with pleasure.

"Must be nice…"

"Oh come on Tonya you know about it."

"Please, Mr. Reid you know I'm here every day." Tonya replied.

"Sure you are. I probably won't be in tomorrow. So I will see you Thursday."

"Alright, have a good day."

"You too," Mitchell said as he walked toward the elevators. He realized Andrea had not called. He began to think that maybe it was him, hoping and wanting her to care more than she really did. As he exited the elevator, towards the front entrance he decided to leave all thoughts of Andrea at the job and in the elevator.

It seemed like the four o'clock break would never come but when it finally did Andrea rushed to the break area to use her cell phone and call Mitchell. Andrea dialed her husband's work number anxious to hear his voice again. "GBS... This is Tonya."

"Good afternoon Tonya, this is Andrea. May I speak with Mitchell please?"

"Mrs. Reid you missed him by thirty minutes. He's left the office for the day."

"Okay thank you Tonya." Andrea hung up the phone very disappointed. She wanted to ask Tonya for the number to reach Mitchell after hours but she didn't want to put her in their business and she wasn't sure Mitchell would appreciate that, then of course there's that company policy bullshit. Well maybe he would contact her...at least she hoped he would.

Chapter 30

Mitchell woke up feeling as though a truck had hit him. After leaving work yesterday Mitchell went to Macys at Stone Crest mall and bought a pair of slacks, a pair of sneakers, and some underwear. He then stopped at Dudley's on Evan Mill road and had a couple of shots of Crown, which had become his drink of choice. Mitchell was feeling pretty good as he left the club and headed towards home. He stopped at the liquor store and picked up a fifth of Crown Royal before going home. Mitchell had already decided that he would not be going to work tomorrow so once he got in he sat in the den and continued to drink while waiting for Darien to come in.

Darien got in that night after 9:00 and took a seat in the den with Mitchell. They sat up late into the night drinking and talking. Darien sat up with Mitchell in spite of the fact that he had to rise for work early in the morning. Darien knew his friend had to be worried about the outcome of tomorrow's hearing. Therefore Darien didn't mind sitting up with his friend and allowing him the time to get some shit off his chest. Mitchell and Darien talked about everything except Andrea. Not one time did Mitchell mention Andrea's name, which was very unusual for him when normally she would be the main topic of conversation. He felt he needed to ask. "Mitchell, what's going on? Usually all you want to talk about is your wife but you haven't mentioned her one time tonight."

"I know Darien. Today I decided to be real with myself. I thought she would have called to check a brother but that didn't even happen. But I bet she will call on the 15th for that damn money. I just don't want to set myself up for the kill."

"Yeah but you've got to understand where she may be coming from man. You are going to court tomorrow for sleeping with her sister…younger sister. What do you expect?"

"I know." Mitchell replied humbly.

"It's a lot to ask of a person Mitch. Any other woman would have had your ass in divorce court the next day. At least you have one that sincerely takes her marriage vows to heart. I can't even say I would be man enough to do that, can you?" Darien asked.

"I doubt it." Mitchell said.

"Come on dawg…" Darien said demanding Mitchell to keep it real.

"Yeah you're right. I couldn't do it either." Mitchell said as he thought about it.

"Just be patient man, if she hasn't served your ass with papers yet give her time." Darien said jokingly.

"I know. It's just that I guess I wanted her to call so badly. In my mind I think I felt like if she called then that would mean our marriage still had a strong chance and that she had forgiven me for my fuck up."

"You've got to forgive yourself Mitch. It happens. We all fuck up. But just learn from it. Pussy is good but it is not everything." Darien said.

"You sure about that…" Mitchell laughed trying to lighten the conversation.

"Okay it is everything, I can't live without it." Darien smiled going along with Mitchell.

"I understand what you're saying." Mitchell replied sincerely.

"All I'm saying Mitchell is when it comes down to it, pussy is just pussy."

"I disagree, Darien there is pussy and then there is *pussy*." Mitchell said.

"You're sick man but you're so damn right." Darien and Mitchell realized that the Crown had taken over their conversation. They laughed until their stomachs hurt. They had one more drink before retiring to their own space. As Darien walked down the hall he turned to Mitchell and said, "Mitchell, just give Andrea some time, don't write her off yet. So what she didn't call, remember she wasn't the one who fucked up man."

"I know."

Chapter 31

The phone continued to ring loudly as Mitchell rolled over in his bed. "Who in the hell is ringing this damn phone so early in the morning?" He felt as though he had just laid his head down to rest on his pillow. It was 2:45 in the morning before Mitchell and Darien

Indiscretions of a Married Man

had decided to call it a night. He wondered did Darien make it in to work. The phone stopped ringing as Mitchell peeled himself from his bed. He walked down the hall to check on Darien, his door was still closed. He looked outside and saw Darien's truck still parked in the driveway. "Well I guess he didn't make it in either." Mitchell said as he found his way back to his bedroom. He glanced at the clock on his way down the hall and it said 12:05. "Damn is it that late?" It took Mitchell a moment to realize it was Wednesday and his hearing was at 9:00 this morning. Most likely it was over, he picked up the phone and heard the short beeps, which was an indication of messages waiting. As he looked at the phone he was a little nervous about checking the messages but he did.

There were five messages and Mitchell hurried through the first four. It was the fifth message that was for him. It was the voice of Ray asking him to return the call as soon as he received the message. He gave no indication on whether it was good news or bad. Mitchell replayed the message three times trying to determine from Ray's voice tone whether it was to be good news or bad. After the third time he still could not determine what Ray was going to tell him so he decided to call. Mitchell sat on the bed for a brief moment, he got up and walked down the hall, stood on the balcony for a minute, deciding to have a cigarette, which he rarely did, he was not a smoker but he felt the need to have one before this call.

Mitchell dialed the number and waited for Ray to pick up. It felt as though little butterflies were dancing in his stomach. His nerves were shot and had caused him to have to use the bathroom, but the phone was ringing in his ear so he had to put that on hold.

"Drake and associates, how may I direct your call?"

"Good afternoon, may I speak with Mr. Drake please?"

"Which Drake would that be sir?"

"Oh I'm sorry, Ray Drake please." Mitchell said.

"No problem, please hold."

Mitchell's stomach continued to knot up as he waited for Ray to come on the line.

"Good afternoon, Ray Drake speaking."

"Ray, how are you? This is Mitchell."

"Very well, thank you and you?"

"I'm not really sure Ray, that's going to depend on what you have to say."

"Then I'd say that you're feeling pretty good."

"Okay. Please tell me something good." Mitchell pleaded.

"Mitchell, they did exactly what I thought they would. They settled for a lesser charge, aggravated assault. Her parents went into shock once we began to divulge all that we had on their sixteen-year-old daughter. They did not want to go to trial and have their daughter exposed as a whore. They would have lost the trial. The Judge in so many words let them know that it would get pretty ugly for their daughter in court. Their attorney tried to paint an innocent picture of Monica and make you seem like the rapist waiting in the woods ready to attack. It may have worked if I had not gathered all

Indiscretions of a Married Man

that I did on her." There was complete silence on the other end of the line. "Mitchell, are you still there?"

"Yeah, I'm just in shock and so happy that I don't have to go to trial."

"No, there will be no trial but you will be on probation for a period of four years."

"Four years! Are you serious?"

"Yes I am. The Judge would not settle for anything less. Although the charges were reduced due to her colorful past, she's still a minor. So I think you made out pretty good."

"When is this probation supposed to start?"

"You will need to report to the probation office on Tuesday morning at 8:00."

"Damn!" Mitchell swore.

"I'm sorry Mitchell I did the best I could."

"Don't be sorry I appreciate all you've done Ray. Thank you for everything." Mitchell said.

"Well if you have any other questions please call me."

"Will do, take care and again thanks." Mitchell said relieved.

"Oh, I thought you'd want to know that your wife was there." Ray said.

"What did you say?" Mitchell asked not sure of what he'd just heard.

"I said I thought you would want to know that your wife was there."

Indiscretions of a Married Man

"Was she?"

"Yes but after I disclosed her sister's past she quickly left the court room."

"Thanks." Mitchell said as he hung the phone up. Mitchell wondered what Andrea's presence in the courtroom was about. She would have heard both sides of the story, details of that weekend that he purposely left out to avoid inflicting more pain. Mitchell sighed deeply as he wondered if what his wife heard in that hearing would help mend or destroy what was left of their marriage.

Once Mitchell hung the phone up he sat on the bed wondering how his wife felt. He wondered if she would ever be able to forgive him. Well she hadn't called since going to the hearing this morning. Mitchell wasn't sure whether that could be considered good or bad. After trying to rationalize his wife's feelings, Mitchell decided to call her on her cell phone. Maybe she would answer the phone, he hoped she would anyway. Mitchell dialed Andrea's cell number and waited to see if she would pick up. He was ready to hang up after the first ring so sure she would not answer the phone knowing it was him on the other end, thanks to caller ID. As he prepared to disconnect the call he heard the phone pick up.

"Hello," Andrea answered.

"Hello, Andrea?" Mitchell never expected her to pick up the phone, but she did. He wasn't sure what to say now, what his reason was for calling?

"This is she."

Indiscretions of a Married Man

"It's Mitchell."

"Yes I know this is you Mitchell."

"How are you?"

"I am okay… and yourself?"

"I feel a lot better after speaking to Ray. He said that you were in court this morning and I just wanted to make sure you were okay. I also wanted to apologize for all that I have put us through." The line was silent. "Are you still there?"

"Yes I am still here and yes I did go to the hearing today."

"Andrea may I ask you why you went to the hearing this morning?"

"I went because I couldn't get in touch with you the day before the hearing."

"You tried to call me on Tuesday?" Mitchell asked.

"Yes Mitchell but you had already left for the day."

Mitchell felt flutters in his stomach as he realized that they still had a chance to recover from this. He immediately realized his wife was one hell of a woman. It took a hell of a woman to support her man in a situation like this. Most people would have called her a fool. Andrea was a strong woman and she did stand by what she believed was right. He could not understand why she was still there. Their marriage was good until six months ago. Even that wasn't a major issue, it could have been put back on track but after what he has done he felt as though their marriage would never be the same.

Indiscretions of a Married Man

He had done the unthinkable; the unforgivable, how could his wife still be there?

"I didn't expect for you to show up in court. To be honest I thought you were done with me." Mitchell said.

"I would love to be done with you Mitchell but my heart keeps butting in."

"Well then I am thankful for your heart. Andrea do you think maybe we could have dinner together sometime?" Mitchell knew she would decline but he had to try.

"Sure we can Mitchell. I'd like that."

"You think it could be next Friday?" He said pushing it.

"I don't see why not."

"Shall I pick you up at 7:00?" Mitchell asked filled with excitement.

"7:00 is good." Andrea answered

"I'll see you then."

"Okay then." Andrea smiled as she slowly hung up the phone. She went to the hearing this morning to give Mitchell some type of support because he had no family here. She also felt she owed it to herself to hear both sides of the story according to the law, a neutral. What she heard in the courtroom this morning about her younger sister completely shocked her. She knew her sister was promiscuous but she had no idea her sister was the person Mitchell's attorney painted her to be. They even had a woman testify that she had to threaten Monica to stay away from her husband. The woman looked older than she did. As Andrea listened to the attorney her parents had representing Monica she thought of walking out of the courtroom. He had painted such an ugly picture of her husband and had given every detail of their lovemaking weekend. The person he described was not the man she married and had lived with for the past three years. At least that was what she wanted to believe. She went to the restroom and was prepared to exit the courthouse but Andrea turned around and went back determined to hear what Mitchell's attorney would say. She wasn't prepared for what she heard and neither were their parents but she knew it was every bit of the truth. She realized her sister played her, she never had any intention of watching cable television, her mission for that weekend was to fuck Mitchell and she had succeeded. Of course, Mitchell was not free of blame but Andrea was now able to put together exactly what happened that weekend. Her husband never had a chance. When she told Monica it was okay for her to spend the night she may as well have said you have my permission to go to my house while I am not there and fuck my husband. Andrea felt nauseous. As Andrea listened to Monica's account of what happened, tears rolled out of her eyes because she now realized her younger sister had set her and her husband up. Andrea then left the court without ever looking back.

Chapter 32

Indiscretions of a Married Man

Mitchell felt a little nervous as he pulled into the driveway to pick up Andrea. He had not been back to the house since he moved out, nor had he seen Andrea since that day. He hoped he wasn't making a mistake by inviting her out to dinner. He did not want to relapse, especially since it had taken him some time to realize they were not going to live up under the same roof any time soon. He asked Darien for his opinion about his date with Andrea. "I think you'll be okay man just stay grounded. Don't go to her with high hopes and set yourself up for disappointment if it doesn't happen. Just put your guard up and enjoy yourself." Darien always kept it real and that was what Mitchell appreciated most about their friendship. He got out of the car and rang the bell, which felt strange. He wasn't feeling too comfortable coming back to his home as a visitor. Although he still had his house key, he would never use it without Andrea's permission. The door opened and there stood Andrea. "Hey." Andrea whispered as she opened the front door wider.

"Hey Andrea, don't you look very nice."

"Thanks, come on in I'll be ready in a second. Can I get you something to drink while you wait?"

"Yes, please." Immediately after Mitchell came in he felt very uneasy and was beginning to think that maybe this wasn't such a good idea. He thought he should have met her somewhere out. This was an awkward situation and he didn't like it. "On second

Indiscretions of a Married Man

thought I think I'll pass on the drink. I'm going to wait outside if that's okay."

"Sure, are you alright Mitchell?" Andrea asked with genuine concern.

"I'm okay I just need a little air."

"I know this is kind of uncomfortable for you because it is for me. If you want to change your mind I would understand."

"No I wouldn't dream of that. I'll be outside." Mitchell walked outside and took a deep breath as he remembered how they used to be.

Andrea came out shortly after him. They began their drive very quietly, each not knowing what to say to the other but both very hopeful that this would be the first step towards repairing their marriage. "So exactly where are you taking me to eat?"

"I thought we could go to Rays on the River."

"That sounds good, I've heard they have very good food and that's a spot we've never been to." Andrea said feeling like she was on her very first date.

"There are a lot of spots we've not had the pleasure of visiting."

"Yeah..."

"Well I blame myself for that. If I had not been so overbearing we could have gone to quite a few places." Mitchell said admitting to his fault.

"Don't blame yourself Mitchell it was both of us."

Indiscretions of a Married Man

"Thanks for taking some of the blame but I do recognize it was my insecurities that put trouble in the water. I was stubborn, selfish, and jealous. I had no life and I wanted you to sit around and have no life as well." Andrea made several attempts to interrupt him as he verbally beat himself up, but Mitchell wouldn't have it. He felt as though this was something that he really needed say. Mitchell had taken time out for self-evaluation and he saw things differently now that he had a life. Darien was teaching Mitchell how to enjoy himself.

Mitchell and Andrea rode to the restaurant enjoying the quiet time in each other's presence. They let the conversation simmer in their minds. Once they arrived at Rays on the River, it changed the entire mood setting. It was such a romantic spot. Mitchell had chosen the perfect place for this date. They began their evening with a couple of cocktails, which relaxed them both enough to have pleasurable conversation. It had been such a long time since they were able to enjoy each other they'd almost forgotten how good it was. They laughed, joked, and enjoyed the bottle of wine Mitchell ordered with their dinner. "Is everything alright for you?" Mitchell asked hoping she was enjoying this as much as he was.

"Everything couldn't be better."

"I'm glad, because I feel the same way." Mitchell said.

"Mitchell, when I sat in that courtroom last week I heard a lot of things that made me realize Monica had a plan and that plan was to get you in her bed. I gave her the okay to spend the night while I was out of town."

"But I allowed her into our bed Andrea and that is wrong. I was wrong."

"You allowed her into our bed because I used sex to control our situation. When I was angry with you I cut the sex off, and then I remained angry and the sex became non-existent we were having. She played us both Mitchell. You are right you were wrong, but I now understand how all of this came to be."

Mitchell was surprised by Andrea's statement. It seemed as though she had taken time to do a self-evaluation on herself as well. He was quite impressed because she was never one to admit guilt very easily. Mitchell was not aware that Andrea had been using sex as a punishment weapon. He just assumed that she had lost interest in it. "I guess we both have had a little time to think about a lot of things." Mitchell said.

"Yeah I guess we have." Andrea said as she smiled at Mitchell.

They continued to enjoy the evening over their meal and even on the way home. They had so much more conversation returning than when they were coming. Mitchell pulled into the driveway and prepared to walk Andrea to the door. They sat in the car for a moment before Mitchell got out of the car, walked to Andrea's side and helped her out of the car. He walked her to the front door. "Well I had a wonderful time tonight."

Indiscretions of a Married Man

"I did too. Would you like to come in for a night cap?" Andrea asked.

"Sure. I'd like that." Mitchell said but was pleasantly surprised.

Andrea opened the door and told Mitchell to make himself at home while she kicked her shoes off at the door and went into the kitchen to get their glasses. "Is cognac okay?"

"That's fine."

Andrea sat down on the couch next to Mitchell and poured their drinks. They talked about a lot of things. They drank and laughed late into the night. Andrea invited Mitchell to stay the night and he immediately accepted the offer. They retired for the night together in the same bed and they made love to each other for most of the night like their lives depended on it.

Mitchell was the first to awake, his head felt a little heavy but his heart felt very light. He looked to his right and saw Andrea lying next to him, as he remembered their night. He smiled as he remembered his wife telling him repeatedly how much she loved him. Was she speaking in the heat of passion and alcohol or was she speaking from her heart. He had begun to give up on their getting back together or him coming home. Now he was sure they could work this out after last night.

Mitchell glanced at the clock and realized he needed to be getting up and getting home because he and Darien had planned to go to the races in Alabama with a couple of the boys. They wanted

Indiscretions of a Married Man

to get an early start so that they would have plenty of time to bet on the dogs. Mitchell eased out of the bed to the bathroom to shower. When he came out of the bathroom Andrea was awake. "Good morning baby." Mitchell said as he was toweling himself dry.

"Good morning back." Andrea smiled.

"Did you sleep well?"

"Yes and what about you?" Andrea said with a satisfied smile.

"Definitely, I haven't slept that good in quite some time!" Mitchell replied.

"Well I'm glad to hear it. Are you hungry? I'm famished. I thought that we could run out and get some breakfast."

Mitchell looked at Andrea as she crawled out of the bed heading toward the bath. It was already ten o'clock and they were supposed to be on the road by eleven this morning. He was sure Darien was up and ready to go, wondering where in the hell he was. "As much as I would love to baby I am running behind schedule. Darien and I are going to the races." He saw a look of disappointment on her face and then that look quickly turned to a look of surprise.

"Oh, I see." Andrea tried to hide the disappointment in her voice but she knew she could not camouflage her facial expression. She was also surprised that after having such a wonderful evening together they would not spend this morning together. She waited to see if Mitchell was going to change his plans but it did not seem he would which was surprising to her. Mitchell continued to get dressed. "A couple of the guys, Darien and I planned this a week ago. I've never been to the races so it should be pretty nice." Mitchell said excited about the trip.

"I just thought that we would spend the day together after such a nice evening."

"I'm sorry baby but I can't back out now, besides I'm kind of looking forward to. I've never been." Mitchell said as he thought of how nice it was to know that she wanted him to stay and he was okay with leaving. "Wow, I've come a long way", he thought to himself.

"I understand. Well I hope you guys have a great time." Andrea tried to sound excited for him. Mitchell was completely dressed, he heard the disappointment in her voice but he was sure she'd be okay because he was not about to change his plans. Mitchell walked over to Andrea embraced her with a passionate kiss and began to make his way down the stair toward the front door. "I'll give you a call baby when I get back."

"Okay be safe and I'll talk with you when you get back." Andrea stood in the door with her robe pulled as she watched him get into his car and pull away. Well at least she knew where he lived and that he had an after work hours phone number. As she made her way back inside Andrea thought aloud, *"Life must be good at Darien's!"* and she closed the front door. Andrea prepared to shower and wash off their lovemaking from the night before. She realized that the Mitchell she'd asked to move out a couple of months ago was not the Mitchell that walked out of there this morning and she wasn't sure why, but that worried her.

Chapter 33

As Mitchell drove away from the address he once shared with his wife, Andrea. He was feeling very proud of himself. Yesterday evening when he arrived to pick her up he was so nervous his stomach became upset. He eventually calmed himself down through dinner but when it was time to end the evening he became nervous again. Andrea invited him in for a drink to end the night and he was so excited. He didn't think that he would end up being there all night. He had fallen asleep so many nights to the fantasy of being able to make love to his wife once again, after that they would work it out, he would move back home and everything would be fine.

Up until last night it was his only fantasy but now that they had actually spent the night together he realized that moving back into the house was not something he desired at this time. He enjoyed the time they had shared last night tremendously but he had also begun to enjoy the freedom he had fought so hard against. Andrea asking him to move out was the best thing she could have done for him. It made him get a life, which was something he did not have before. He still loved her and wanted their marriage but he had gotten used to being out here by himself and Darien had taught him how to enjoy himself and he liked it.

Darien was packed and waiting when Mitchell came through the front door. "What's up man? I thought you'd changed your mind." Darien looked at Mitchell wondering if he had weakened any after spending the night with Andrea.

"No way, I'm looking forward to this little outing."

"Seeing that you're just getting in I'm going to assume that you're date with Andrea went well." Darien said.
Mitchell smiled and nodded his head as he said, "It was pretty nice."

"You'll work it out?" Darien asked trying to get a feel for how Mitchell was feeling.

"She wanted to spend the day together."

"You could have bailed out man, I would have understood." Darien said.

"Believe it or not, it was nice but I'm not ready to move back in. I realize a lot has happened and thanks to you I've also learned how to enjoy myself again but I need time. Like she needed time, I need it now. It's a slow healing process, now I understand what you were saying. It's not something that happens over night. I realize cheating strips trust and it takes no time to lose it but it takes forever to get it back. I just think it's too soon." Mitchell said feeling very strongly about what he just said to Darien.

"You think she's ready?" Darien asked.

"No. To tell you the truth I think once she sat in that courtroom and heard all that was said she accepted the thought that maybe I was seduced by her sister and that I'm not just some stray dog out to get a nut. She kind of blames herself for allowing her sister to spend the night while she was away from home. Who does that, Darien?"

"Yeah for real, what woman would do that shit?"

"My damn wife..." Mitchell laughed lightly as he grabbed his bag.

"Well you know you're home and you don't have to go anywhere."

"I know and thank you for that brother. Well enough of that, let's go and have some fun." Mitchell said.

As Mitchell and Darien were about to head out the door, Darien noticed Mitchell didn't have any change of clothes, "Mitch, you got everything because I think we may stay over."

"Thanks for letting me know." Mitchell said walking toward his bedroom.

It took him no time at all to put a few personal items in his bag. As they walked out the front door, Mitchell thought how nice it felt to pick up and just go.

Chapter 34

Indiscretions of a Married Man

Andrea showered, dressed and decided to visit with her parents today. It seemed as though it had been such a long time since she had went over and sat with them. Before this mess she visited them at least once a week. She had stopped visiting because of Monica but why should her relationship suffer with her parents because her younger sister's act. Andrea was ready to put this behind her and it started last night with Mitchell.

Although Mitchell had elected to go to the races with his boys she felt good about last night. Last night she found peace within herself about Mitchell and Monica. Now it was time to resume her visits with her parents and put her life back in order. As Andrea approached her parent's home she wasn't quite sure if she would be able to deal with Monica just yet but she needed her relationship with her parents.

Andrea and Monica stood face to face at their parent's front door. They had not spoken to or seen each other since the preliminary hearing. Andrea had partially prepared herself for this today but Monica was caught off guard. When she opened the front door and her sister stood there her first instinct was to quickly close the door before she tripped on her again. But she didn't because Andrea seemed very calm. "Hey, are mom and dad here?" Andrea asked.

Indiscretions of a Married Man

Monica looked awkwardly at her sister because she expected her to say nothing at all to her. "No, but they should be back in a few if you want to wait."

"Yeah maybe I'll wait. Do you mind?" Andrea asked.

"No I don't mind." Monica said as she moved to the side and Andrea stepped through the door. It seemed a little uncomfortable as the two stood in the foyer facing each other. Each was not sure what to say or if they should even say anything at all. "Well I'll be upstairs." Monica said deciding to make it comfortable for the both of them.

"Monica, you think we could talk for a minute?"

"…Only if you promise not to lock any doors or attack me." Monica tried to make light of the situation.

"I promise." Andrea smiled. The two walked into the den and sat down across from each other. They sat for a brief moment in silence before Andrea spoke. "They say time heals all wounds and I am a believer of that. I've had time to sort things out and put some things into perspective. Although I don't understand why, I forgive you and Mitchell. You are my sister and I love you. Mitchell is my husband and I love him. I don't know if I'll ever trust you or him again but I am willing to try." Andrea said with sincerity.

"Andrea I cannot tell you how sorry I am. I was stupid and I wasn't thinking. I never met anything I said the last time you were here." Monica paused for a brief moment. "I don't expect you to trust me, but thank you for not hating me." Monica said earnestly with relief. She really missed her sister.

"Well I will tell you I came damn close." Andrea joked because she didn't want this conversation to get any more serious than it already was. She was tired of being mad at everyone and just wanted her life to go back to the way it was. Funny that she still believed that it could.

As Ben and Helen Brown entered their front door they heard voices coming from the den. The voices sounded familiar but it would have been too good to be true that they were the voices they sounded to be. Ben and Helen looked at each other as they approached the den and saw their two daughters sitting together laughing as they had in the past. It was truly a moment that they thought they would never witness again.

"What have we done to deserve this wonderful treat?" Ben asked as joy filled his eyes.

"Hi dad..!" Andrea jumped off of the couch to give her father a warm hug. She then turned to her mother, "Mom!" she said as she reached over to hug her as well. Monica remained seated on the couch as she watched her sister and parents embrace. She was so happy that they could finally try to restore their family after her what she and Mitchell had done to them.

"It so good to see you baby," Ben said not remembering when the last time his family had sat and enjoyed each other. They sat for two hours laughing and talking about little things.

Indiscretions of a Married Man

"Well I've got to be going." Andrea could have stayed all night but she remembered Mitchell was supposed to be back from his trip with the boys tonight and she really was looking forward to spending some of the night if not all with him.

"You don't have to rush off baby." Her mother said half convincing. Andrea knew under normal circumstances her mom would have been in the bed before ten and dad following shortly thereafter.

"No mom I need to be going." Andrea hoped that they would not ask any questions because she was sure it was a little too soon to explain to them that her and Mitchell had spent last night together and that she was trying to see him tonight. Andrea got up from the couch and found her shoes so that she could head toward the door. Monica rose from her seat to walk her sister to the door. She reached out to hug her sister as she spoke, "Andrea I love you sis…" Andrea was taken aback because Monica had never said that to her with such sincerity. "Monica I love you too." She really meant it.

"I really want you to know I made a big mistake Andrea and I will never do anything to ever hurt you or our family again." Monica said as tears welled up in her eyes.

"I know Monica, I know." Andrea hugged her before walking out of the door. Their parents had decided to give them a moment alone, aside from the fact that they were too relaxed to get up from their comfortable seats. "I love you mom and dad, see ya'll later."

"Bye baby." They both said in unison, looking at each other, knowing just what the other was feeling. They had been together just that long.

Chapter 35

Andrea drove towards home feeling pretty good about her day as she went over the day's events in her mind. Her parents were as happy to see her, as she was to see them. She had not expected to say much to Monica but she did and she was glad about that as well. Monica seemed genuinely sorry for all that she had caused, it seemed as though this entire episode had changed her. Maybe her attitude change had to do with the fact that Debra's father would not allow her to deal with Monica after he overheard their conversation, the conversation that had changed all of their lives in one way or another.

Andrea pulled into her driveway excited to get inside and check the messages. She was sure Mitchell would be on the answering service. She could not believe how excited she was about seeing him. Just a couple of weeks ago she could not even imagine making love to him ever again. Andrea immediately went to the answering machine after entering her home. There were no messages; the message light was not blinking. She sat in the den for

Indiscretions of a Married Man

quite some time and tried to figure out why Mitchell had not called. He said he would call when he got back into town. After sitting for a while she decided to call him. The phone rang but there was no answer. She decided not to leave a message. An hour passed and Andrea's phone had not rung, she decided to call Mitchell back, this time she decided to leave a message. "Hey Mitchell, this is Andrea its 11:30 and I haven't heard from you. I thought you said you were going to call when you got in. Where are you?" As soon as Andrea hung the phone up she knew she should not have asked where he was, she didn't have that right anymore. "Damn why did I do that?" she asked herself disappointedly. Andrea sat a little longer before she began to think of nothing else except why Mitchell had not called her and why had she left such a message on his answering service. She decided she needed to get out. There was no way she could sit here the rest of the night sulking and it was Saturday night too. At first she thought to call Sharon but she knew there was no way Sharon was coming out of the house past 11:00 at night but Dee would. Andrea found her phone book and dialed her number. Dee picked the phone before the first ring was completed, she must have been expecting a call. "Hello."

"Hey Dee, this is Andrea."

"Hey Andrea, what's going on girl?"

"Not a damn thing I am bored as hell and was looking for something to do." Andrea replied.

"You are kidding me right?" Dee asked.

Indiscretions of a Married Man

"No I'm dead ass serious. What are you getting into tonight?"

"Well I really wasn't going to do anything but I started getting bored my damn self."

"You want to go somewhere?" Andrea asked.

"Where are you trying to go girl. You know you are shocking me because you don't call my ass ever, at least to go out anyway. I thought you had stopped going out."

"I had but I'm ready tonight. So what's up you down?" Andrea asked.

"Are you coming to get me?" Dee asked because she knew if she went out this late she was going to get her drink on and doubted very seriously if she would be coming back home tonight."

"Where are we going?" Andrea asked.

"What about Taboo? I heard it is really nice." Dee replied.

"Yeah we can go there, okay, I'll be there in 20 minutes." Andrea

"You must be dressed already."

"Yeah I am. See you in a minute." Andrea knew it would take her at least 30 minutes to get dressed but she couldn't tell Dee that because she wouldn't be ready when she got there. It had been a long time since Andrea had went out so this should be pretty nice.

Andrea pulled in front of Dee's home forty-five minutes later but she was sure that Dee would be ready and she was. They got to Taboo's at one o'clock in the morning and they were still jamming.

Indiscretions of a Married Man

Andrea felt a little out of place once they had gotten inside because she had not been out in a while. She went directly to the bar, it was standing room only but she didn't mind. Dee ordered the first round of drinks, two shots of tequila. Andrea did not drink tequila and she wished Dee had asked her what she preferred before she assumed tequila was okay. Since Dee had ordered and paid for this round of tequila Andrea would drink it. They clicked their glassed and tossed their shots back. "It doesn't taste as bad as I thought it would taste." Andrea stated.

"Girl, watch it, that Patron will put something on your ass." Dee warned Andrea.

"I got the next round when you're ready."

"I'm ready." Dee said.

"...Already?" Andrea knew she shouldn't be trying to hang with Dee. She was an expert at this compared to her being quite the amateur. Andrea flagged the bartender and ordered the next round. They shot them down. After that Dee wanted to walk the club. "Let's see what's up in here?"

"Dee I can see from here, you go ahead I'll be right here when you get back from sightseeing." Andrea said.

"Okay but you don't know what you're missing."

"I'll pass, all I need to see I'll see from right here." Although the club had thinned out a little bit, Andrea was not trying to sweat from walking around. A man finished his drink and got up from his seat at the bar and she immediately sat down. Feeling a little

Indiscretions of a Married Man

uncomfortable sitting at the bar without a drink, Andrea decided to order another one. She decided to stick to drinking the tequila because she wasn't a heavy drinker but the one thing she had always heard was don't mix your liquors. She sat and watched the crowd, the DJ was jamming and she was swaying to the music. "Would you like to dance?" the voice came from behind her.

Andrea's reflex said, "No," before she could turn around and properly address the man asking.

"Well the way you're moving in that seat I was so sure you would say yes."

Andrea smiled as she turned to see who the man was. He stood over her at 6'5 definitely eye candy and there was a lot of that in here.

"I would dance but I'm not ready to give up my seat and have to stand the rest of the night." Andrea just knew that would deter him. He politely turned to the lady sitting next to Andrea and asked, "Would you mind watching this seat while we dance?"

"Sure, no problem..." She said and he grabbed Andrea's hand leading her to the dance floor. At first Andrea felt a little awkward but after the first couple of steps it seemed the tequila slowly made its way into her blood stream and relaxed her enough to enjoy that dance and a couple of more songs before she retired from the dance floor. Once returning to her seat, the gentleman followed her and planted himself on the side of her barstool. The music had been too loud for them to do any talking. "What are you drinking?" He asked.

"Tequila…" Andrea replied.

"Hanging with the big boys huh?" Andrea had no clue what he was talking about but she assumed the drink was one to be careful with. She just smiled and he ordered them a round of tequila. "I'm Rodney and you are?" He asked.

"I'm Andrea."

"Please to meet you Andrea. You sure know how to move on that dance floor."

Andrea blushed as she watched the round of tequila being delivered in front of them. They talked for quite some time and Andrea found out more than she chose to know about him for the night. But it was pleasant conversation and he was very entertaining. It seemed the drinks never stopped coming and Dee had shown her face once since they had gotten to the club. Apparently she had found a candidate and was going in for the kill. Andrea already figured out that Dee probably would not be leaving with her, which was one of the reasons she didn't go out often with her because it was always a manhunt for her. Andrea decided to slow down on the tequila since she'd probably be leaving alone.

Chapter 36

Indiscretions of a Married Man

After the dog races they hung around, sure that there would be entertainment in the evening but it was not, so they decided to return to Atlanta. They got into Atlanta at one o'clock in the morning. Darien and the others were feeling a little restless and did not want this Saturday night to go to waste. Mitchell had thought about going back to the house and getting his car, going to see his wife. But after looking at the clock he decided he would just wait until tomorrow, maybe they could have a quiet Sunday afternoon. Darien's voice interrupted Mitchell's thoughts. "Man you feel like partying a little bit?"

"It's one o'clock man. Where are you trying to go?" Mitchell asked.

"Well let's hit Taboo, they jam until closing." There were three other guys in the car and they seemed to be in agreement with the choice so Mitchell figured why not, he had already blown the night with Andrea.

They pulled into Taboo's parking lot and it was still pretty packed. They exited the Durango truck and entered into Taboo. It was still a crowd and they were jamming. Mitchell was not in the mood for the drinking so he located a corner in which he felt comfortable and that was where he stationed himself and watched the crowd while Darien and his other three partners roamed the club. Mitchell had been asked to dance several times and had turned the offers down until Tracy stood in front of him. "Thank you for the call." She said with a drip of sarcasm.

Indiscretions of a Married Man

"I'm sorry. I've just..." Before Mitchell could finish the sentence Tracy interrupted him. "Please Mitchell don't say anything, you'll only make it worse."

"Okay, then I will take your advice." He said as he looked at her, she seemed much more attractive than he had remembered.

"Thank you." Tracy said very dry.

"Are you sure I can't explain myself?" Mitchell asked not wanting to seem like he was full of shit.

"Okay, give it your best shot." She wasn't mad with him, she just enjoyed seeing him squirm.

"Truthfully I'm not ready for anything. I separated from my wife a short time ago and I'm just not ready."

"Mitchell it was only a call." Tracy said appreciating his honesty.

"Yeah, to you it was only a call but to me it was a little more." He smiled and was glad she did not make an ugly scene. These days' women were just as vicious as men were when it came to rejection.

"I understand, more than you know. Would you like to dance?" Tracy asked.

"Sure why not." Mitchell led Tracy to the dance floor. They danced through three songs before the music slowed down with the Tyrese single, *"Shame."* Mitchell was prepared to lead Tracy off of the dance floor but she grabbed hold of his hand and held him there. Mitchell placed his arms loosely around her waist and they began to dance very slowly to the music. They danced through that song and of course the disc jockey followed up with an old school hit by Keith Sweat *"Make it Last Forever."* Mitchell closed his eyes for a little while during the second song and immediately thought of Andrea, he pulled Tracy in a little closer to him. As the song was close to its end he opened his eyes, looking at the couple dancing to the front of him, they were wrapped up very closely and looked as though they were very much into each other.

"It doesn't take a rocket scientist to figure out what they are doing when they leave here tonight." Mitchell thought. The song was over and the lights slightly came up, Mitchell glanced again at the couple that was wrapped so tightly on the dance floor as they made their way off the floor and his mouth dropped to the floor. The woman looked identical to his wife. He practically forgot about Tracy as he moved quickly through the crowd trying to catch them as they exited the dance floor. Mitchell got right up on them and tapped the woman on the shoulder. Before she even turned to face him, he knew it was Andrea. She turned around to see who was tapping her shoulder and for what, she certainly was not trying to dance again. As she turned she was not prepared for the face that glared at her, it was Mitchell. Andrea stood stiff in shock she did not take another step. Mitchell glared at her so intensely it seemed as though he was looking straight through her. Andrea noticed that there was a very attractive woman standing closely behind him as though she were with him. He said nothing, he just walked off of the

Indiscretions of a Married Man

dance floor and the woman followed. They exchanged a few words, embraced and Mitchell walked through the exit door. It suddenly seemed as though the club were suffocating him. Andrea tried to reach for him but he was moving too fast. Andrea walked quickly out of the club behind him. He was standing in the parking lot on the side of the club. She walked up to him but he would not even acknowledge her, he continued to stare straight ahead.

"Mitchell..." Andrea called his name in almost a whisper. He would not answer. She said nothing for a minute and tried again. "Mitchell..."

He turned and looked at her in complete silence. Andrea saw what she thought was pain in his eyes. "Mitchell, please say something."

Mitchell looked Andrea deep in her eyes not knowing exactly what to say without going off on her. He couldn't understand how she could be on the dance floor wrapped up with a complete stranger after the night they had spent earlier. "Andrea now is not a good time. Please go back inside and continue to enjoy your dance."

"Mitchell what are you talking about? What's the matter with you and who is that woman you were with?"

"Nothing is wrong with me. Please go back inside!"

"Why? What have I done? Who was the woman Mitchell?" Andrea pleaded.

"Andrea, don't play Miss Innocent with me!"

"What in the hell are you talking about?"

Indiscretions of a Married Man

"You just don't get it do you?" Mitchell couldn't believe she was standing in front of him acting as though she had no clue to what he was referring.

"Get what?" Andrea screamed.

"Damn! You are amazing! Did you enjoy the fucking dance? Just what the hell were you doing on the floor? Why didn't you just go home and fuck him?"

Mitchell had lost complete control. He could not believe that his wife was out in the street letting strange men grind up on her. What the hell was she thinking? He thought they were making progress after the night they had spent together. He felt like a fool, he had spent the entire trip with his boys thinking about getting back with his wife. He was not ready to move back home yet but he truly believed because he was not trying to date or be with anyone else Andrea would be doing the same. From what he had seen on that dance floor he had never been so wrong. His wife was closer than close with another man on the dance floor and there he was trying to put as much space between him and Tracy as possible. He just didn't understand and now here she was playing innocent or was she…he wasn't quite sure. Maybe she wasn't as ready as he thought she was. Andrea's voice snapped him out of his thoughts. "What in the hell is that suppose to mean?"

"Andrea you were all up in the man's grind! We are still married you know!"

"Why in the hell are you tripping Mitchell?"

Indiscretions of a Married Man

"Oh, I'm tripping because I don't think that it's okay for my wife to be all wrapped up on the dance floor with someone other than me... her husband! Well excuse me."

"I don't believe you!" Andrea said.

"No! I don't believe you!" Mitchell yelled.

Mitchell began to walk off from Andrea towards the truck and then realized he couldn't get in. He decided to go back into the club and let Darien know he was leaving, he could not stay there, and he would take a cab if he had to. As he walked off Andrea followed him calling for his attention. "Mitchell I do not understanding what's going on. If I have done something that has offended you, please tell me so that we can address it now." Andrea decided to reason.

"Don't worry about it baby." Mitchell said as he continued to walk toward the entrance of the club. There really was nothing Andrea could say right now that would change the way he now thought of her. Seeing her on that dance floor grinding up against another man took something away from him.

In the months that had passed, damn near all he fantasized about was to be with her, *his wife,* no other had touched her since he had been with her. The thought of another man, no, the sight of another man grinding into his wife just took the sacredness away.

"Damn, why'd you have to be here tonight? You fucked everything up!" Mitchell said and walked into the club not once looking back at her.

Indiscretions of a Married Man

Andrea stood there wondering what the hell just happened. True she was a little impaired by the alcohol but she wasn't drunk. Why was Mitchell tripping she wondered. All she did was dance and he made it seem as though she had gotten naked on the dance floor and fucked. Andrea continued to replay the last hour in her mind and eventually she realized that the guy she was dancing with, Rodney was his name, was all on her. But it was just a dance and even though she had allowed Rodney to get carried away she had to make Mitchell understand that it meant nothing to her, it was just a dance. She wanted to be with him, especially tonight and she couldn't afford for anything to screw that up. They had been through enough already. She wasn't sure that their relationship could take much more and survive. She entered back into the club to find him and make sure he understood it was him she wanted and no one else before he got away for the night. If he did, chances were they would never be able to work it out, she couldn't risk it.

Mitchell looked around for Darien and finally located him on the dance floor. He seemed to be enjoying himself. Mitchell didn't want to be the one to break up the party, the club would be closing in another hour or so and he was sure he couldn't stand that. Maybe he would locate Tracy and dance the rest of the night away, good idea but not what he felt like doing. Mitchell thought about Andrea on the dance floor with another man, and his stomach began to turn. He knew he had no right to act the way he was after sleeping with her sister and going to jail for it. But they were past that, this was about something else. He loved Andrea and the thought of another man holding her tight enough to smell her did something to him, she was his wife. He went to the bar and ordered a double shot of Crown as he turned from the bar to return to his corner he ran right into Andrea. "Mitchell I need to talk to you, please don't turn away." She ordered another shot of Tequila. Mitchell stood and waited to hear what Andrea had to say. He noticed she ordered Tequila, he had never seen her drink that. What did she know about Tequila? She barely drank. That might explain why she was out here like that. "Andrea what are you doing out here alone? And when did you start drinking Tequila?"

"I came out with Dee." She answered.

"Oh shit, I should have known. Why would you come out with Dee? Where is she?"

"She's around here somewhere. I waited for you to call and you never did. I left a message and when I didn't hear from you I decided to go out with Dee."

"I just got back into town. I thought it might have been too late to call you so I went with the guys. They wanted to come here and that's what we did. I get in here and see my damn wife all twisted up on the dance floor with another man."

"Mitchell please, it wasn't like that."

Mitchell just looked at her, he could see in her eyes that she was quite toasted and although he was angry with her right now she was pretty amusing. It had been a long time since he had seen her

Indiscretions of a Married Man

like this. She certainly was in no condition to drive, he needed to find Dee, and most likely she had already found her a one night man and left. He needed to make sure Andrea made it in safely if he had to drive her home himself. As Mitchell and Andrea talked he was convinced she was a little more than tipsy, they danced a couple of songs and then he began to search for Dee. He had no luck locating Dee it seemed she had vacated the premises. He then located Darien and let him know that Andrea was in no condition to drive home, Dee had left her and he had instantly become the designated driver.

Mitchell took Andrea's keys and escorted her to the car, she slightly stumbled but it was okay because she was with him and nothing was going to happen to her now. As he drove towards what used to be their home he thought of all they had been through and wondered how something could go so wrong so quickly. He didn't wonder for too long because he knew he was the reason. That was something he still had a problem taking credit for.

Andrea sat in the passenger seat knocked out as he pulled into the driveway and parked, he took a moment to admire her beauty even in her drunken state. "Baby we're home." Immediately after the words left his mouth Mitchell realized what he had said. "Thank God she's out." Mitchell said as he prepared to help Andrea out of the truck. He knew this was where he would lay his head tonight and although he would love to make some serious love to her, he refused to take advantage of her being intoxicated even if she was his wife. "Andrea, wake up baby." Mitchell said as he lightly shook her.

"Mitchell, are we home yet? I think I may have drunk a little too much tonight. Did Dee get home okay?"

"Yeah she got home." Mitchell really could have given less than a damn if she got home right about now. She sure didn't care about his wife. Not even enough consideration to let her know she was leaving. Mitchell helped Andrea to the door, used his key to open the house and escorted her upstairs to what was their bedroom at one time. Andrea was mumbling something, but Mitchell couldn't decode it. He sat in the chair and stared at her, a smile came to his face. He couldn't believe she was toasted, he had not seen his wife like this in years.

After sitting for a moment Mitchell decided to get her undressed so that they both could get a little rest before the sun came up, it was already 4:00. He walked over to the bed and began to undress Andrea. He undressed her to her underwear, what little she was wearing. She had on a lacey red thong and no bra. Mitchell immediately became aroused. He wanted to take her thongs off, part her legs and taste every inch of her but he decided not to take advantage of her even though she was still his wife. Mitchell pulled the comforter and sheet back to place them over her. Afterwards he undressed down to his underwear; he didn't think Andrea would mind that they slept in the same bed. He turned out the light and slid between the covers trying not to touch Andrea because he needed to calm down, he was already aroused. He laid in the bed remembering how he felt seeing another man put his hands on his wife and he made up his mine that they were going to work through this and be together because that was one thought that didn't set well with him.

Just as Mitchell began to drift into a deep sleep, Andrea rolled over crossing her leg upon his. He assumed she was still asleep until she began to slowly grind against his thigh. She eased on top of him and her mouth found his, she passionately kissed Mitchell. Her mouth began to travel down the length of his body taking Mitchell's penis in her mouth. A soft moan escaped from Mitchell's lips as his body slowly began to rise and fall from the bed. When Mitchell could no longer take it he gently pulled Andrea up from him and laid her on her stomach. He started with a kiss on her neck and continued down her back on to her feet. He then rolled her over and kissed her ankles; his kisses traveled up Andrea's legs and stopped right below her belly button. Andrea reached down and lightly ran her fingers through Mitchell's hair. She did not want him to stop, what he was doing to her felt so good. Andrea called out Mitchell's name several times before she arched her back in complete satisfaction. Just when she thought it could get no better, Mitchell covered her body with his and he entered her. Mitchell and Andrea made love throughout the night until they were both completely exhausted. Mitchell listened to Andrea's light breathing as she slept. He quietly lay in bed savoring every moment of the lovemaking they had shared. Mitchell remembered the time they were in bed like this and him waking up the next morning to his wife inviting him to leave. He wondered what surprise awaited him come this morning. Whatever it would be he was sure it could be no worse than the last time he was in this bed. With that thought he drifted off to sleep.

Chapter 37

Mitchell and Andrea slept well into the afternoon. They showered, ordered in Chinese food and slouched around in the den for the most part of the day. Not wanting anyone to interrupt the private moment they had going on, they hear a car pull into the driveway. Andrea looks through the blinds to see her father's car pulling in. "What is he doing here?" She asked herself aloud. It was unlike her father to pop up unless it was something urgent. His timing was less than perfect.

"Who is it baby?" Mitchell asked.

"It's my dad."

Mitchell's face got tight, he had not seen any of Andrea's family since the shit with Monica and he wasn't sure he was ready to see them now especially her father, he was the last person Mitchell wanted to see. He knocked on the door and Andrea seemed to be in no rush to answer the door. "Would you like for me to leave or go upstairs?" Mitchell asked quietly.

"Why would I ask you to do that?" Andrea replied.

"If you're not ready to deal with this, I don't mind." Although Mitchell asked, it was he who was not ready to deal with it.

"No Mitchell I'm an adult and I am at home, he will just have to deal with it. It's no better time like now." Andrea got up and answered the door. Her father stepped in and hugged her like he always did. "Hey baby, I was in the area and thought I'd stop in and just remind you that the family is coming in from Long Island this weekend for the reunion so don't make …any…plans…." He was having trouble finishing his sentence once he noticed Mitchell sitting in the den quite comfortable.

"How's it going Mr. Brown?" Mitchell humbly asked, not expecting much conversation from Andrea's father.

After staring at Mitchell for what seemed like an eternity, he turned towards his daughter, "What in the hell is he doing here?" Ben asked his daughter ignoring Mitchell completely.

"He's here because I invited him." Andrea replied with a little attitude.

"Why would you invite this man back into your life? He has disrespected our entire family and you are sitting up in here with him like he hasn't done a goddamn thing!" her father yelled.

Indiscretions of a Married Man

"Please dad I really don't need this right now." Andrea tried to remain calm with her father. She knew he would not be happy about seeing her and Mitchell together but she had no idea he would be this vocal. Mitchell remained silent as he sat on the couch, not wanting to irritate Mr. Brown anymore than he already was.

"I can't believe you would act this desperate! This man has slept with your 16-year-old sister! Did you forget that?" He was screaming to the top of his lungs.

"No I haven't forgotten that dad but this is my business…" Andrea answered, trying to maintain respect.

"No it became our business when that horny bastard sitting over began fucking his way through the family!" Her father continued.

Mitchell rose from the couch having heard all he could stand. "Mr. Brown I can only apologize to you and your family for what I have done…"

"Don't you say a damn word to me, all of the apologies in the world will not fix what you have done o my family!" He spit out as he began to walk up on Mitchell, finally able to confront him about what he had done to his daughters. He wasn't about to let this opportunity get by him. He walked up to Mitchell, preparing to put his hands on him. Ben Brown had waited for this moment for quite some time. He grabbed Mitchell by the collar of his tee shirt, drew his fist back and punched him before Mitchell knew what happened. Andrea jumped in front of her father to prevent him from hitting

Indiscretions of a Married Man

Mitchell again. Mitchell refused to swing back on her father, he felt he deserved it, if it were his daughters he would have done the same thing. He couldn't blame him but he wasn't about to let him hit him again. Mitchell yanked himself free from Andrea's father, located his belongings and walked out the door leaving Andrea and her father standing there.

While driving home Mitchell tried to rethink a few things out. As soon as he got into the house the phone rang, he knew it could only be Andrea.

"Hello." He answered trying to conceal his anger.

"Mitchell?" Andrea whimpered.

"Hey. Are you alright?" Mitchell asked.

"That's why I was calling you to see how you were. I'm so sorry. If I had known my dad was going to act like that I would have never let him in."

"It's okay, he's your father and I understand how he feels. I would probably have done the same thing." Mitchell wasn't sure Andrea understood that just because they were willing to work this thing out did not mean everyone would be accepting of it. That was what he needed to make her understand. "Andrea the one thing you are going to need to realize is the fact that your family will never accept me back into your life."

"Well it's not up to them Mitchell, it's between me and you." Andrea said.

Indiscretions of a Married Man

"I understand that but they are your family and I don't want you to have to choose baby. Family is very important to everyone." Mitchell tried to explain.

"I'm not choosing Mitchell. They will always be my family as you are my husband."

"Okay I just want you to think about this because it can become very uncomfortable for you and me."

"Mitchell I love you and I want this to work, my family will just have to deal with it." Andrea said adamantly.

"Okay I just want you to be sure." Mitchell said and they continued to talk late into the night before finally retiring.

The week went by fairly smooth, Mitchell seemed to be spending more time at the house with Andrea than at Darien's place, which was now considered his home. He had slept at his previous home with Andrea almost every night for the last three weeks and although it seemed nice and cozy, Mitchell was not quite ready to give up the comfort of knowing he had his own place.

He was surprised Darien had not given him a hard time about it. As a matter of a fact Darien had asked him two weeks ago if he still lived there. He explained to Darien that he was not ready to move back in with Andrea yet. He loved his wife and would not trade her for the world, but he wasn't ready to pack it up. He was not ready o give up his new found single life. Darien let Mitchell know that there was no pressure in moving out and if he wanted to be there during the day and with Andrea at night that was okay with him. Mitchell really appreciated Darien's friendship, he couldn't have asked for a truer friend.

Mitchell and Andrea had not talked about him moving back into the house but he knew it was coming. Andrea seemed to be enjoying the time they spent together and Mitchell had assumed that she would grow tired of his company after a day or two, but she had not and quite frankly he had began to look forward to coming over and spending his nights with her. It was nice falling asleep with her warm body next to his. That was something he thought he'd never get to enjoy again but she had decided to give them another chance and for that he would always be grateful.

Chapter 38

Andrea sat at work watching the clock anxious to get off. Mitchell bought tickets a play at the Fox Theater. Andrea just loved the Fox because it was such a classy place to hang out at. Andrea hated the fact that it wasn't the weekend but nonetheless she was looking forward to them getting out together. They had spent every day together since Sunday, despite the fact that her father had interrupted their cozy Sunday afternoon with some very ugly behavior.

Indiscretions of a Married Man

Having Mitchell's body beside hers at night was comforting, she missed that. Their relationship seemed to be so much better and Andrea asked herself, "Is this what it took, for us to communicate and enjoy each other once again?" Mitchell seemed to be pretty comfortable himself. He made sure he called her before leaving work so that they were on the same page once their workday was over. Normally Mitchell met her at the house when her shift was over. This became a little inconvenient for them both. So being that she was on the evening shift and he on days, she suggested, he just let himself in and she'd see him when she got home. Mitchell agreed and it seemed to be working out pretty well.

The ringing of the phone on her desk interrupted Andrea's thoughts. "Andrea speaking, may I help you?"

"Andrea? This is mom."

"Hey mom, what have I done to deserve this call?" It was unlike her mom to call while she was at work unless it was something that couldn't wait until she got home, so she wondered what it was her mother had to say.

"Well I thought you'd like to know that your dad's family has gotten in from New York this morning for the reunion. I thought you may have forgotten since we had to reschedule the date from three weeks ago. They are here and want to see you baby. I'm frying up some chicken and catfish with Cole slaw and corn tonight, think you can make it over?" Her mom asked.

Indiscretions of a Married Man

"I can't tonight mom, I have a previous engagement." Andrea was glad her father had not called. She had not spoken to him since Sunday. He made it very clear that he disapproved of her and Mitchell. She was glad Mitchell had chosen to leave because her father held absolutely nothing back. He voiced his feelings from way back when he disapproved of their marriage. Andrea realized he was her father but some things should just be left unsaid.

"Oh really... Good for you! What about tomorrow or Saturday? Tomorrow we're going to out to eat and Saturday if the weather allows we are going to Stone Mountain to grill." Her mom said.

"I'll try to make tomorrow. Okay?" Andrea said.

"You must have a pretty busy schedule. I'm glad to see that you're getting out. Where are you going tonight?" Her mom questioned.

"Mitchell and I are going to the Fox Theater to see the play tonight." The phone went silent and Andrea knew it was just a matter of seconds before her mother began her sermon. At least she would be subtler than her father would.

"Did you say Mitchell?" her mom said.

"Yes mom I did." Andrea said as she prepared for battle.

"It's been three weeks since your father told me that he was over there. Are you two back together?"

"Mom we are working through our marriage." Andrea said.

Indiscretions of a Married Man

"Really... Do you hear yourself?" Her mom asked astonished by what she was hearing.

"Yes I do and I've heard dad and now I'm hearing you!" Andrea yelled.

"No need to get hostile."

"I'm just sick of hearing it mom. He's my husband and if I choose to be with him after he's cheated that is my business." Andrea said.

"Even after he's cheated with your younger sister." Her mother asked.

"Whatever." Andrea replied with much attitude.

"You can watch your tone Miss."

"I've got to go back to work mom." Andrea said suddenly.

"Well I want you to know that the family is looking forward to you coming and I expect you there at least one of the four days." Her mother demanded.

"I'll be there."

"I don't think it would be a good idea to bring Mitchell." Her mother said quietly but firmly.

"Well what else is new mom? Dad has made it very clear that Mitchell is not welcomed to anything that our family has. It's very uncomfortable for me to come to Sunday dinners and other family gatherings without my husband."

"Well Andrea, I hate to say this but he made that choice!" her mother replied finally raising her voice.

Indiscretions of a Married Man

"I bet you do. Bye mother." Andrea hung the phone up abruptly almost forgetting it was her mother on the other end of the phone. Andrea sat for a moment trying to regain her composure. She couldn't believe how her parents tried to dictate her life. She had never really noticed it until this mess with Mitchell and Monica. Well no one would tell her when it was time to give up on her marriage. She would just have to show her parents that she was no child; she would have to show everyone.

Chapter 39

It was the end of the week, "Thank God for Friday!" Andrea said out loud as she thought about what a wonderful evening they had. The play was excellent and they enjoyed it tremendously. All afternoon her thoughts had been of how great their relationship was. It almost seemed as if they were newlyweds and she was not about to complain.

Andrea decided to take her break and try to catch Sharon before she left. Since she'd been on second shift she had not been able to catch up with her at home or at work. Just as she was turning the corner to the break room, which was on the second floor she

Indiscretions of a Married Man

caught a glimpse of Sharon going into the break room. "Hey there stranger..!" Andrea said, glad that she had finally caught up with her.

"Andrea, what's going on sister?" Sharon asked.

"Not much. How are you my friend?"

"You know me, I'm not a complainer. I am just trying to get out of here. I heard you and Dee went out a couple of weeks ago." Sharon said.

"Big mistake girl, big mistake. You know she left me at the club without saying a damn word." Andrea said.

"Yeah that's how Dee rolls. That's why I go nowhere with her." Sharon said.

"Well now I know."

"So how's everything else Andrea? You look good, got a man in your life yet?"

"As a matter a fact I do." Andrea said, preparing herself for another battle.

"Go ahead then sister with your bad self!" Sharon was a little surprised with Andrea's answer she had not expected her to say yes. "Well who is he?" she asked with excitement.

"It's Mitchell, Sharon. We've decided to work on our marriage and it's been good." Andrea answered and waited.

"I should have guessed that." Sharon totally disapproved but did not want to taint her friend's decision. She did not understand how she could do it. It was one thing for a man, your husband no doubt, to cheat but to cheat with your under aged sister was a little more than she could understand but that was Andrea's decision and she would have to live by it. She didn't know too many women who could. "So it's you and Mitchell... huh?"

"I know you don't approve Sharon but I have to try." Andrea said.

"Whether I approve or not shouldn't matter, what should matter is that it is your life and you have to live with your decisions, no one else. If you like it, I love it girl! Do your thing. Now I've got to clock out I'll call you this weekend." Sharon said.

"Okay, but I won't hold my breath." Andrea left the break room and returned to her work desk. She sat down at her desk and smiled lightly at the conversation she and Sharon just had. "Sharon was so full of shit. I know she can't stand the fact that I'm with Mitchell but she sure talks a good one." She thought as she continued to smile before her phone line rang. "Andrea Reid speaking how may I help you?"

"Hey baby, you sound so damn professional." Mitchell said as he smiled into the phone.

"Thank you! Now what can I do to you, I mean for you?" Andrea smiled.

"You had it right the first time. You know exactly what you can do to me..." Mitchell said.

"Why don't you refresh my memory when you get in tonight?"

Indiscretions of a Married Man

"That would be more than my pleasure." Mitchell said as he enjoyed the conversations that he and his wife had lately. So what time are you going to get home tonight?" He asked.

"I hate to tell you, but I'm sure it will be the same time it was last night and the night before that and the night before that…" Andrea said.

"Okay, I get it when your shift ends." Mitchell knew she got off the same time every night and got home at 12:15 every night he just asked out of habit.

"That's right. What do you have planned?" Andrea wondered if he was beginning to get bored with her company. She hoped not because she was really enjoying his, so much that she thought about approaching the subject of him coming back home. She thought about waiting for him to confront it but he had not. Maybe he was just waiting for her to bring it up and what better night than tonight.

"No plans baby except to wait for you to get off." Mitchell said.

"Are you going to be at the house?"

"I'm not really sure. I think I may go by the house and check on Darien. I haven't spent a night home in about three weeks. I'd like to check on him and let him know that I'm still alive and make sure he is." Mitchell said.

Andrea felt a slight sting hearing Mitchell refer to another place as home. Yes, tonight she would approach the subject. She needed to let him know that he could not have the best of both worlds. They were going to be together under one roof or not and if not then he needed to stop cock blocking by staying over every night. "Well you know my dad's having his family reunion this weekend?"

"I know. That was one reason why I thought I would go by Darien's so that you would have the freedom of participating without feeling obligated to make sure I'm going to be okay." Mitchell said.

"Mitchell I can do both without you having to go."

"That's not what I'm saying baby. What I mean is I want you to have a good time without worrying about me."

"So are you coming by tonight?" Andrea asked.

"I'm not sure. I'll probably just go by the house and pick up a couple of things."

"Mitchell I want to talk to you about something." Andrea said.

"What is it baby?"

"I'll wait until tonight."

"Come on Andrea, you know I hate when you do that. What is it baby?" Mitchell asked.

"Don't you think it's time for you to come back home?" Andrea asked boldly.

The phone went silent for a moment before Mitchell's voice came back on line. "You're right baby. We'll talk when you come in tonight." Mitchell said, thrown aback.

Indiscretions of a Married Man

"What is there to talk about Mitchell? You're there every night anyway."

"We'll talk about it tonight baby, okay?" Mitchell knew this was coming but he had expected it to come this soon. Now that he was confronted with it, he wasn't sure what he wanted to do. He enjoyed being with Andrea. He would have it no other way but he had become so secure with knowing that he had his own place across town. Realizing if he said he wasn't ready, that would probably terminate their relationship. Yet he knew that he didn't want to move back yet. He was going to have to think of a way to prolong this conversation. Who would have thought it would be him that was not ready.

"I guess it will have to be okay." Andrea wondered why he was so hesitant about moving back home. He was there every night anyway.

"I'll see you tonight baby." Andrea was silent. "Andrea?"

"Yeah I'll see you tonight." Andrea hung the phone up and returned to work. She was distracted for the rest of her shift with the fact that Mitchell was hesitant about moving back home. Well one thing was for damn sure, he was going to make a choice tonight and if he chose not to move back home then they would have to rethink this little arrangement they had going on. She would not continue to spend every night with Mitchell while he held on to his little rest haven in Darien's home. If he chose to remain at Darien's then she would have to choose to move on without him. And she really hoped it would not come to that although everyone else did.

Chapter 40

Mitchell sat in the den at the house Andrea was now asking him to move back into. He was not sure why he wasn't ready to come back home. It was not like he was dating other women or partying every night. After sitting a while longer searching for an answer within himself he realized that his fear of going back home was because he felt as though their relationship would change and go back to the way it was before he cheated. The boredom, the arguing, the rationed sex, and all the other bullshit that they both endured before, he did not want to go back to that. He enjoyed the way they were now and he didn't want anything to change. He loved his wife more than anything but he was sure he wasn't ready.

Mitchell went upstairs to the bedroom and began to gather his dirty clothes and a couple of other items he had accumulated there. He decided he would spend the night at Darien's, which he now referred to as his home and hopefully that would buy him a little time before he sat down with Andrea and talked about it. He knew that once they sat and talked he was going to have to commit to doing it and he wasn't ready to do that tonight. Mitchell decided

Indiscretions of a Married Man

to call home and see if Darien had anything planned for the evening. Maybe he would hang out with the crew if he could catch up with them, but if he couldn't he would sit at home alone tonight and make sure he knew what it was he was doing. Darien never answered the phone but it was still pretty early. Mitchell decided to have him a nice shot of Crown on the rocks and relax until traffic died down. Rush hour traffic was bad enough but on Fridays it was unbearable, almost enough to give you a serious case of road rage. He continued to sip on his Crown while he watched Def Comedy Jam on BET. He slipped into a very comfortable sleep and when he woke it was eleven forty five at night. "Damn Andrea will be here in a minute! I need to get my ass up and get out of here before she gets home and pins me up." Mitchell grabbed his bag and raced towards the front door. Once in his car and a couple of blocks away from the house he relaxed a little bit. He felt pretty bad about what he was doing but he didn't want to be forced into a move he might not be ready for. So to help ease his conscious he decided to stop in DUGANS sports bar on Memorial Drive and have a drink before going home. Mitchell's one drink turned into three drinks and two hours later. It was after two o'clock before Mitchell walked out of the bar and drove towards home.

    He pulled into the driveway and quietly eased through the front door. He noticed Darien's truck outside and didn't want to wake him; it seemed pretty dark inside. As Mitchell closed the front door he noticed soft music playing, it was the jazz sounds of Najee.

Indiscretions of a Married Man

The lights were nice and dim so Mitchell decided not to turn any on. He assumed Darien had finally gotten him a lady over here. No wonder he had not been able to catch up with him lately, some woman had his time twisted up. He didn't want to bust the mood Darien had going on. He knew Darien wasn't expecting him so he decided to tip past Darien's room towards his own.

As Mitchell approached Darien's room he noticed the door was not closed completely and the room was barely lit up by the night-light Darien kept plugged into the wall. Mitchell stopped and tried to decide whether he should make his presence known or just tip past the room. He decided, to keep embarrassment down he would just tip past the room. Just as he was stepping past the door trying not to look in he heard a low moan, on reflex he glanced into the room and his jaw dropped to the floor. He could not take another step, he was frozen in place. Mitchell blinked his eyes to make sure he was seeing correctly. Darien was at the edge of his bed on his knees naked with his ass out and someone was stroking him from the back. This someone did not have breasts, they had a dick! Mitchell stood in the doorway for what seemed like forever, but it was only a few seconds of watching his friend having sex with a man. They were so into it they never even noticed he was there. The way they were moaning Mitchell thought Darien was giving some woman the best sex ever but he was wrong it was Darien getting it like a woman. Once Mitchell came out of his trance, he quickly stepped to his room, shut and locked the door behind him. As Mitchell sat on the bed, he asked himself, how could he not have known? The entire time he was there no woman had ever called there for Darien nor had one came by but Mitchell just chalked it up to his partner being picky. Never in a million years would he have thought it was because his friend wanted to be with men instead of women. Mitchell wanted to get the hell out of there but he didn't want to have to walk past that scene again so he remained in his room devastated. Devastated that the one true friend he had liked men. Mitchell could not understand how this could have happened. He knew that he could not stay there, first thing in the morning he was out. For Mitchell this changed a lot of things, it especially changed his earlier thoughts of not being ready to move back home. If he wasn't ready before tonight he certainly felt a sudden change of heart now. Mitchell tried to remain awake but he drifted off to sleep with the image of his best friend Darien being penetrated by another man.

Mitchell awoke to the bright sun shining through his bedroom window. It was morning and it could not have come fast enough. Mitchell rose from the bed and packed enough clothes to carry him through the week. He exited his room hoping he would not bump into Darien. He was not ready for that.

Just as Mitchell grabbed the front door knob, Darien's bedroom door opened. Mitchell tried to open the front door and get out before someone stepped through Darien's door but did not make

Indiscretions of a Married Man

it. "Damn when did you get in?" Darien asked. His voice seemed calm but surprise was showing all over his face.

"What's up?" Mitchell was not feeling him and really did not want to converse with him at all.

"Where are you going with that big ass bag man? And when did you get in?" Darien was very persistent in finding out when Mitchell had gotten in. Unfortunately he was busted and Mitchell felt the need to let his undercover ass know. "I got in late last night." Immediately he saw the tightness in Darien's face and waited for his next question.

"Oh I thought you'd spent the night with Andrea since that has been your routine lately." Darien wondered how late Mitchell had gotten in and had he seen or heard anything. They were quite noisy he thought but that was only because he assumed they were in the house alone.

"No I decided to come on in last night after a few drinks at Dugan's." Mitchell knew Darien was nervous that his secret may have slipped out last night but he refused to make this easy for him.

"So did you have a good time?" Darien asked.

"Yeah it was okay. I needed a little personal time so I stopped in for a drink." Mitchell said.

"Why didn't you holler at me when you got in?"

That was it for Mitchell. He could not play the game anymore. "You were a little tied up brother." Darien's face became stone.

Indiscretions of a Married Man

"What's that suppose to mean?" Darien said.

"Man you know what the hell it means. You could have closed your fucking door last night! What the hell is going on? I thought I knew you but I don't know who you are!" Mitchell yelled.

"What in the hell are you talking about?" Darien knew what Mitchell was talking about but he was prepared to deny this to the end. He was sure Mitchell couldn't have seen too much. "Damn why the hell did he just pop in? He should have called! Now this was going to be ugly he could see it already," Darien thought to himself. He wanted to tell Mitchell when he moved in but it wasn't necessary because he wasn't dating anyone. He hadn't started dating until three weeks ago and he had seen no reason to tell Mitchell, he wasn't there half the time anyway, he was sure it would have been a matter of time before Mitchell moved back in with Andrea. He was over there every damn night why had he come home last night.

"Let's cut through the damn chase here Darien. Last night you left your door open and I saw your ass bent over for a man!" Darien couldn't say a word his mouth fell open. "So you are speechless now? Your ass was crying out like a little bitch last night!" Mitchell spit out.

"Watch your mouth Mitch!" Darien said, ready to swing.

"What the hell are you going to do? Punk ass…!" Mitchell didn't want this to get ugly but he just could not understand how his best friend whom he had bonded with over the years was a homosexual. He had heard rumors in college that Darien was bisexual and on more than one occasion his name had been linked to other football players caught in compromising situations but they had spent a lot of time together and he was so sure his partner was all man. He had witnessed him getting down with the ladies, he didn't understand and he was not ready to accept it.

Darien was instantly in Mitchell's face and the space between them had become very tight. "Regardless of what you think of me, I still have the strength of a man and will give you a run for your money so I'm only going to say it one more time, watch what you say!" Darien really didn't want to fight Mitchell but he was not about to let him stand here and disrespect him. "I know you don't want to hear what I have to say and you probably think that I'm fucked up. What you saw last night wasn't meant for you to see but you did and I'm sorry if you don't agree with my preference but I am still the same Darien you've always known. Nothing has changed Mitchell, nothing."Darien said.

"I beg to differ. I'll be back for the rest of my things." Mitchell walked through the door closing it behind him. He got in his car and never looked back.

Chapter 41

Indiscretions of a Married Man

When Mitchell arrived at the house Andrea was not in, he decided to let himself in with his key. He carried his bag inside and sat down on the sofa in the den. He turned nothing on as
He sat consumed with the thought of Darien being gay. He couldn't erase the image of last night. Hearing it was one thing but to actually see his best friend being penetrated by a man was a little more than he could handle. He didn't understand why and he really wasn't sure he wanted to. He thought long and hard until he eventually drifted off to sleep.

Mitchell was awakened by Andrea's jeep pulling into the garage. He felt too exhausted to greet her at the door and wondered how long he'd been asleep. Andrea saw Mitchell's car in the driveway as she pulled up and wondered what storm dragged him in. He was approximately 18 hours late and she couldn't wait to hear why. She entered the house through the garage, which led to the den. There lay Mitchell on the sofa in complete silence. Andrea noticed that he did not have the television or the stereo on. She immediately assumed that something must be wrong because whether he watched the television or not he always turned it on to keep him company is what he had said. Mitchell looked up from the sofa at Andrea and she saw that something was definitely wrong. "Are you all right baby?"
Mitchell stared at her for a short while and she quietly waited for him to answer the question. His look seemed far away as though he

was not even there. "Baby is everything okay?" Andrea asked as she noticed the big bag placed at his feet.

"No everything is not okay Andrea," He answered. She was beginning to worry about what was disturbing her husband and growing impatient.

"Well what's wrong Mitchell?"

"I want to come back home," Mitchell asked in monotone.

Andrea was confused. "I thought that was what we were supposed to talk about last night but you didn't show."

"I stopped at Dugan's to have a drink and ended up being there longer than I had planned."

"You could have called Mitchell. I don't think that is asking too much, do you?"

"No Andrea it is not. I was a little intoxicated and it was closer to drive to Darien's house than here."

"Once you decided you weren't going to make it here, was the phone to far to reach as well." Andrea asked.

He realized Andrea wanted to argue but he was not feeling it. He did not want to take out his frustration and anger out on her and say something he could very well regret. "No. I was not thinking about calling once I got in. The only thing I wanted to do was to lie down."

Andrea looked at Mitchell and realized he was in a mood, he didn't sound right. He sounded as though he had no fight in him and she was sure that now wasn't the time she should push. "Baby why don't you go upstairs and get some rest, are you hungry?"

"Yeah a little, what time is it?" Mitchell asked.

"It's six o'clock."

"You've got to be kidding." Mitchell had slept most of the day away and he felt as though he had been up all night. He had a restless night and a rough time going to sleep knowing that in another room his best friend was having sex with a man. He couldn't tell Andrea about it because if he did then she would realize that was the only reason he decided to come back home and that would create more problems than it was worth. She didn't need to know everything and he really didn't believe she needed to know about Darien being gay, at least not now anyway. Mitchell thought to himself how much he needed to rest after such a mentally exhausting night.

"I think I will lie down for a minute." Mitchell said as he walked towards the steps. They had not even discussed his moving back in but it seemed to be what Andrea wanted and there wasn't much to discuss unless he decided to bring up the Darien incident and he was not about to do that. As he walked to the bedroom he decided that if Andrea didn't bring it up neither would he. He just wanted to move forward. And with that thought Mitchell dozed off into a deep sleep.

Andrea relaxed in the den to the thought that her husband was back home. Normally she would have given him a bad time and not have made it so easy for him but the look in his eyes seemed to tell more than he was. She knew Mitchell was a no nonsense man so she decided to leave it alone but she could not deny the happiness she felt in her heart that he was back home.

Chapter 42

Everything seemed to be going well since Mitchell had come back home. It had been almost two months of honeymooning and Mitchell couldn't complain about anything, all was lovely with the exception of Andrea's parents. Initially when he moved in they would call, he'd answer the phone and they would say nothing, he'd just catch a dial tone. He had brought it to Andrea's attention so many times and nothing changed so he finally decided it was what he would have to deal with as long as they were back together. In the beginning they thought that with time it would pass but her family was not backing down, they made everything hard and uncomfortable. It seemed as though they put in time and a lot of thought into making their life miserable. They would constantly invite Andrea to family functions and make sure she knew he was not welcomed. Every Sunday they would call and ask was she coming to Sunday dinner. Andrea didn't know whether to say yes or no. It was as though she was straddling the fence and wasn't sure which side of the fence she should stand on. It had become very annoying and it was beginning to affect their relationship. Mitchell sat back and tried to think of a quick fix, he had spoken to his dad about what was going on with him and Andrea. His dad suggested they take a weekend to visit in South Carolina. Mitchell told his dad that he knew no one in South Carolina and he wasn't too comfortable with going. That was when his dad informed him that he had cousins in South Carolina. He told Mitchell to call back tomorrow and he would have the phone numbers for him.

Chapter 43

"Hello may I speak to Denise." Mitchell asked.

"This is she."

"Hey girl this is your cousin Mitchell." It seemed a little funny because Mitchell had not spoken to Denise or her sisters since they had graduated from high school.

"Damn, are you serious, Mitchell what the hell is up?" Denise was totally shocked that after all these years Mitchell had called. They had not seen each other since childhood. Why in the hell would he possibly be calling after all this time?

"What's been going on cuz?" Mitchell asked.

Indiscretions of a Married Man

"Not a damn thing. Where did you come from? I haven't heard from you in how many years?"

"It's been a while. I think the last time we saw each other was…" Mitchell said.

"Was when we were kids man, I'm sure it had to be at least ten years."

"Yeah you're probably right."

"I am cousin, I am." Denise said.

Mitchell couldn't believe that it had been over ten years since they had seen or spoken to each other and it seemed as though they hadn't missed a beat, like ten years had not even passed. "Damn girl I didn't know you were in South Carolina, my dad said your sister and brother were there too."

"Yeah they are. So when are you coming?

"I was thinking about visiting this weekend." Mitchell said.

"You know I don't believe you right?"

"I'm serious Denise I am coming."

"When Mitchell, when?"

"I said this weekend?"

"That's great if you are serious." Denise said.

"I am. I'll call you when I'm pulling out of Atlanta, okay?"

"Yeah that's cool. I'll talk to you later, call me cousin." Denise said.

"Okay later Denise."

"Later."

Indiscretions of a Married Man

Two weeks had passed since Mitchell had spoken with his cousin Denise. He and Andrea had talked about relocating and decided to go to Charleston and see what the job market had to offer. In less than a month after talking to his cousin, Mitchell and Andrea were on the road heading towards Charleston, South Carolina.

When Mitchell first approached Andrea about visiting South Carolina she was excited that he wanted to get away for a weekend until he mentioned the fact that he wanted to check things out for a possible move. Andrea was not ready to move from Atlanta until her parents showed their disapproval of her and Mitchell for the last time. They were constantly calling the house and if Mitchell answered the phone, her father would just hang up in his face whereas her mother would not say hello she would just rudely ask to speak to her daughter. When Andrea brought it to their attention they both stood by their thoughts that Mitchell deserved no respect and she may have accepted him back in her life but they would never. They would constantly insist that Andrea come to the house for Sunday dinners and when she did not show, her parents would leave a very ugly message on their answering service. They would come by the house and refuse to come inside if Mitchell was home and refused to acknowledge him at all. It had become quite an uncomfortable situation. Once Andrea realized that this was something that time was not going to heal, she decided that maybe it was best for everyone if they moved away from Atlanta.

Indiscretions of a Married Man

Mitchell and Andrea arrived in Charleston late Thursday night at 2:45 a.m. they checked into a hotel and would give his cousin a call later in the morning. After awaking and checking out of the hotel, they phoned Denise, there was no answer. Assuming she was probably at work they decided to take the afternoon into their own hands. They rode around and enjoyed the sights. They had lunch downtown by the water, afterwards they parked the car and toured a few of the big houses that had been turned into tourist sites, they also got a chance to view the slave block by the water. It all seemed so historical and they really enjoyed it. As they walked along the water everything they had been through seemed nonexistent. Mitchell phoned his cousin at 5 p.m. hoping that she was in. A man answered the phone and introduced himself as Randy, Denise's fiancé. He gave them directions to their house and let them know Denise had not gotten in from work yet but they were welcomed to come.

Mitchell and Andrea found the house with no problem and Randy greeted them at the front door, showed them where they would be sleeping so that they could get a little comfortable before Denise came in. They put their bags in the guestroom and sat out on the deck enjoying the fresh air. Denise got in and although she and Mitchell had not seen each other since they were little kids it seemed as though they had not missed one day. "How long has it been girl?" Mitchell asked.

"I know it's been over ten years at least."

Indiscretions of a Married Man

"Yeah it's been a long time. You've got a nice place here."

"Thanks Mitchell. So you are thinking about moving here huh?"

"Seriously thinking, I got a chance to roam around downtown a little bit and I like it." Mitchell said

."What about you Andrea, what do you think? I know all of your family is in Atlanta."

"So far I like it. There's a lot to see." Andrea said as she looked at Mitchell.

"I can give you a couple of leads on a few jobs, Westvaco is a pretty big company here. Maybe you can get on with them." Randy assured him.

"Are you serious man, I work for a company in Atlanta that is under Westvaco?" Mitchell was then convinced that this move was met to be.

"Why don't you pay them a visit Monday morning and see what they can do for you?" Randy said.

"No doubt," Mitchell could not conceal his excitement.

Denise invited Andrea to the family room for a little wine and a little girl talk since the men were talking shop. Randy decided to light up the grill for a little chicken and steak along with a good salad and baked potato. With everyone in agreement Mitchell and Randy went to the store to get all that was needed to begin their Friday evening.

Indiscretions of a Married Man

The evening was going well. The men bonded outside by the grill and the beer cooler, the women bonded inside by the stereo with the wine. Everyone came together and ate until they could not eat another bite. "Damn baby this sure hit the spot." Denise complimented Randy on his meal. She was full and ready to continue getting her drink on. There was still meat on the grill and the guys seemed to be going nowhere too fast. Denise invited Andrea back to the family room and they sat on the sofa as they enjoyed their wine, they had finished one bottle and were working on their second. Andrea was feeling quite tipsy but she continued to drink. "How long have you been in South Carolina Denise?"

"I've been here for about seven years." Denise responded.

"You must like it."

"It's pretty cool and it's a lot of different things to do here." Denise said.

"I saw that earlier today while we were downtown." Andrea began to slur. Denise was feeling a little light headed too but she just slowed down her drinking.

"So you and Mitchell are ready for a change huh?" Denise asked.

"Mitchell seems to think if we move from Atlanta that will make everything better." Andrea slurred out. Denise wondered what she was talking about but she was not going to ask, she did not believe in prying into others business, including family. She didn't have to ask because Andrea continued as if she had been asked.

Indiscretions of a Married Man

"This is Mitchell's idea to come here. We were separated and we've only been back together two months, if that." Andrea slurred.

"Oh I wasn't aware of that. I'm glad you two were able to work it out." Denise knew Andrea was a little beyond tipsy now because she was telling too much too quick. It almost seemed as though she had been waiting to exhale in a sense.

"That's why we're moving to try and work it out. My family is not making it easy for us. So he thinks if we move here we'll have a better chance."

"Well at least he's trying to ensure you'll have every chance possible of making it." Denise said.

"That's the least he could do since he slept with my sixteen year old sister." Andrea blurted out.

Denise's bottom jaw almost hit the floor. She could not believe what she had just heard. Andrea was so caught up in telling Denise that she failed to see the reaction on Denise's face. Andrea went on to tell her every detail of Mitchell and Monica's weekend while she was in Biloxi. Mitchell and Randy walked in on Andrea explaining how her parents had him arrested; his face instantly turned to stone. He locked eyes with his wife and Andrea paused for a minute before she attempted to continue her story. Denise looked at Mitchell with embarrassment, "I'm sorry," she whispered. Randy looked puzzled as Mitchell walked over to Andrea and suggested that this was not the time or the place.

"Is everything okay?" Randy asked Mitchell.

Indiscretions of a Married Man

"No, everything isn't okay. I was just telling Denise that we're here because Mitchell went to bed with my sixteen year old sister." Randy was not prepared for that. Everyone except Andrea felt the room fill with embarrassment. She still insisted on telling her story but Denise and Randy ended it by retiring from the room, leaving Andrea and Mitchell alone. Mitchell apologized but the damage had already been done, she had tainted their visit before it had gotten started. Mitchell led Andrea to their room and helped her into bed, he knew Andrea had drunk more than she could handle so he blamed her behavior on the drinking.

Mitchell woke up late Saturday morning. It was almost noon and Andrea was still sleeping. Mitchell decided to let her remain sleep. He wanted her to sleep off last night. He heard movement outside of their room and decided now was a perfect time to try and explain with an apology for Andrea's outburst last night. As he opened the door the smell of breakfast drifted up his nose. He peeked into the kitchen where Denise and Randy were at the table eating breakfast. "Good morning." Denise and Randy said simultaneously. "Have some breakfast Mitch." Randy said.

"I'd like to explain last night and apologize." Mitchell said humbly.

"There is no need for an explanation. Whatever the reason you are here that is your business, man. We're still going to help in any way we can." Randy said with all sincerity.

"I appreciate that but I still owe you an apology."

"Apology accepted now sit down and get some of this good breakfast." Randy said.

After breakfast Mitchell showered and dressed before Andrea awoke. Randy invited him to spend Saturday afternoon with him and a couple of his friends. They were taking a boat out to test their fishing skills. Mitchell accepted the invite and was very excited about it. It had been years since he had been fishing and besides that he was not in such a rush to share the day with Andrea after the show she put on last night. Mitchell had been so embarrassed he could barely look his cousin in the face. Andrea had put all of his business right out there for all to see without consulting with him first. He felt slightly betrayed. She had no right embarrassing him like that but thank God that his cousin and her fiancé were not judgmental. He was determined to complete his task here no matter how many monkey wrenches his wife threw. He was determined to move here regardless of whether Andrea accompanied him or not. After last night, that didn't seem to be so important today.

Chapter 44

Their week in Charleston had turned out to be quite successful for Mitchell, he'd interviewed with Westvaco and they

Indiscretions of a Married Man

made him a comfortable job offer, which he was more than happy to accept. He also put a deposit down on a nice two-bedroom townhouse apartment. He completed all the paper work and signed a six-month lease before they left Charleston to return home. He was prepared to leave Atlanta forty-five days from today, which would be one week before his start date at Westvaco. He was really excited about the move, he had a new job and they would be in a new environment where no one knew of their history with the exception of his cousin, thanks to his wife. He would also be around some of his family instead of just his wife's relatives. He had not been around his family in years. Andrea didn't seem too happy about Mitchell inviting her to stay in Atlanta for as long as she needed to. As angry as he was about her running her mouth he was almost ready to tell her to just stay in Atlanta. She embarrassed not only him but also herself with her second outburst about their situation. It seemed that when she drank she wanted to tell whoever would listen about his cheating with her sister.

It happened again, Wednesday night as they all sat on the deck enjoying a little cognac, Mitchell and his cousin Denise reminisced about their childhood while Andrea and Randy listened, sharing in their moment. After a while Mitchell noticed Andrea's attention had diverted from their conversation to her own with Randy. He tried to continue his conversation with Denise but it seemed whatever Andrea and Randy were talking about really had her going. Mitchell decided to listen in to see what had his wife so

Indiscretions of a Married Man

upset. After hearing a small part of their conversation Mitchell wished he had not. Andrea not only had Randy's attention but she now had his and Denise's attention as well. She was giving details of how she felt so betrayed by my act of infidelity. She went on for quite a while before Denise interjected and said, "If you are so upset Andrea then maybe you should move on. Don't forgive him and stay with him just so you can keep bringing the shit up every time you think someone will listen. That is not cool!" I could tell that Denise had become as irritated with this subject as I had. I got up from my seat on the deck and went inside. Only this time it was not I she was embarrassing it was herself. I had heard more than enough for a week about how I betrayed her.

The ride home was uneventful, Mitchell had very little to say to Andrea and she was so embarrassed by her actions that she could not find the words to ask for forgiveness. Therefore Andrea slept most of the way home and that made it a more comfortable ride for both of them. Once they pulled into their driveway Mitchell called Andrea's name to awaken her. Once she was awake he turned towards her and looked at her with disgust in his eyes, "I just want you to know that not only did you humiliate me twice in front of my family but you also embarrassed yourself. You acted like a pitiful drunk!" Mitchell grabbed his bags out of the jeep and went inside without ever looking back. Andrea sat in the jeep for a long time. She felt very bad for what she had said while in Charleston but what was done was done and she couldn't take it back. All she could do

Indiscretions of a Married Man

was apologize and Mitchell walked away so quickly he never heard it.

Three weeks had passed by and they had not been out together once since returning to Atlanta. Mitchell just could not get over the humiliation his wife had put him through and did not want to risk her getting drunk and doing it again. He was still upset about her telling his business but he had forgiven her because he understood that his wife did not drink regularly and when she did drink, alcohol seemed to take its full effect in her. Therefore he would not hold her responsible for her actions.

They had not talked about her outburst since they had returned home. Mitchell seemed to be acting a little cocky since they had returned from Charleston. Andrea knew exactly why he was acting this way but he had no room to be mad about anything she did for the next couple of years considering what he had done and had been forgiven for. Mitchell slept in the guestroom for a week and Andrea just assumed he would get over it because she had and after a week he did.

It was decided that Andrea would follow Mitchell a month later. Andrea told Mitchell that her job asked her to stay for an additional thirty days until they could find a replacement and she had agreed. Andrea knew Mitchell was packed and ready to go. He had agreed to come back and finish the move once Andrea called and let him know she was ready to come.

Indiscretions of a Married Man

The night before Mitchell was to leave Andrea took half a day off from work to prepare a nice romantic evening for him. She wanted this to be a night he would never forget, one that he would remember for the remainder of his life. As Andrea prepared dinner she chilled a bottle of wine that they received on their wedding day. She pulled out the candles that had never been put to use and placed them strategically throughout the house.

Mitchell walked through the front door thanking God it was his last day of work. He had given his notice two weeks ago and was glad this was the last day. As he walked through the door he immediately noticed the candles she had selectively placed throughout the house. He was so impressed with the mood his wife had set he had to tell her about it. Mitchell walked through the house smelling up the dinner Andrea had taken the time to prepare. He found Andrea in the kitchen pulling the chilled wineglasses from the freezer preparing to fill them with wine. "Baby, what has you feeling so good?" Mitchell asked his wife as he continued to look around.

"You baby!" Andrea answered in barely a whisper.

"Just what have I done to deserve this layout?"

"Oh not much yet baby it's what you will do later and about what I'd like you to remember about our last night together."

"What do you mean our last night together baby? Never our last… Just until you get to Charleston. What would you like me to remember about tonight baby?" Mitchell asked.

Indiscretions of a Married Man

"I can show you better than I can tell you." Andrea said in her most enticing voice. Mitchell walked upon her from behind and wrapped his arms around her as he slowly kissed her neck. Mitchell began to grind into Andrea turning them both on. Realizing Andrea had mapped out a long and pleasurable evening Mitchell regained control and went upstairs to shower.

Minutes after stepping into the shower he heard the door open and recognized his wife's naked silhouette. He immediately became excited as Andrea stepped into the shower with him, which was something they had not done in a while. They began to wash and caress every inch of each other's body before exiting the shower. Mitchell could not help but to lead Andrea's wet body from the shower to the bed. He laid Andrea on the bed and lay beside her as he parted her legs and slowly began to massage the most intimate part of her body. He fondled Andrea until she was soaking wet, he then made love to her with his mouth and an intensity that she had never felt from him before. Mitchell had her body on fire and just as she was ready to demand penetration he got up from the bed. "Baby what? Where are you going? I am so ready for you," Andrea said between her heavy breathing.

"We've got all night to finish baby. I've only just begun with you." Mitchell said as he rose from the bed and wrapped a towel around his waist. Andrea lifted herself from the bed in disappointment, refusing to put on anything.

Indiscretions of a Married Man

"Let's have dinner baby so that I can get to desert." Mitchell knew she was more than hot for him and that alone excited him.

There was not much talk during dinner but there was a lot of seduction going on. After they finished eating Andrea grabbed the bottle of wine and instructed Mitchell to follow her up the stairs. He followed her up the stairs into the bedroom with no argument at all. Andrea then made love to him like she had not in a very long time. She wanted him to remember everything about this night for the rest of his life. That was her ultimate goal for the evening. Mitchell moaned and groaned confessing his love to Andrea like he had never before. They made love through the entire night each trying to satisfy the other in every way possible. Totally exhausted they passed out in each other's arms.

Morning came and Mitchell rose ready to go. He loaded his boxes into the mini trailer he had rented from U-Haul, which was attached to the back of his car. Andrea laid in the bed with a smile on her face as she listened to him loading up the trailer. She knew that Mitchell was excited about this move and he couldn't wait to get it started. He felt as though a new environment was exactly what they needed to put their marriage back on track, Andrea begged to differ. It would take more than a new location to repair what his infidelity had damaged. As Andrea continued to lie in bed she heard Mitchell coming up the stairs. He stood in the middle of the doorway with a smile stretched across his face. "Good morning, my lovely wife!" Mitchell said as he strolled over to the bed in cut off blue jeans shorts and a white wife beater.

"Good morning baby." Andrea said as she lay across the bed enjoying the cool breeze across her nakedness.

"You look pretty damn sexy laying there in your best outfit." Mitchell smiled.

"Is that right?"

"It is definitely right." Mitchell said as he made his way to the bed and grabbed his wife in his arms preparing to make love to her before she decided to get out of the bed. "So baby you ready to get on the road?" Andrea asked.

"Not quite yet. I've got to begin this move the correct way. You know what I mean?" Mitchell asked as he covered Andrea's mouth with his before she could respond.

It was noon before Mitchell and Andrea crawled out of their bed. He had gotten so comfortable that he wasn't ready to pull himself away from her. Earlier this morning he was excited to get on the road but now as he lay besides his wife he wasn't sure he wanted to leave her behind. He had gotten so used to having her warm body next to his at night and in the morning. The thought of thirty days without her was not something he was looking forward to.

Chapter 45

Indiscretions of a Married Man

Three weeks had passed since Mitchell left Atlanta and he seemed to be settling in very well. He had begun his job at Westvaco and welcomed the change. Mitchell was on second shift and it was taking him a little time to get adjusted to the hours. It seemed he woke up in time to get ready for work and once he got off of work he showered and went to bed. It didn't help his social life any.

Each night when he got in he called Andrea. Their initial conversations were of Mitchell wanting her to hurry and get there; of how much he missed and loved her. Andrea didn't seem to have much to say. Most of their conversations Mitchell did the talking while she just listened. He repeatedly asked her why she had become so quiet when he called; her reply was always that she was tired. Although Mitchell wanted to believe her, he didn't. He was sure it was more to it than she was telling him. He'd just have to wait until she was ready to talk about it. Their lack of conversation was beginning to make Mitchell very uneasy so he decided to put a couple of days in between the nightly calls to his wife, giving her time to get over whatever was bothering her. He thought it might be that she wasn't as ready for their move as he had been. It seemed that whenever he mentioned how excited he was about her coming she had nothing to say.

A week later Mitchell called Andrea and received no answer, he made several attempts to contact her at home and the phone just continued to ring. When he called her at work he got her answering service. Mitchell began to worry so much that he decided to call his cousin Denise and discuss it with her. She answered on the first ring. "Hello."

"Hey Denise, what's going on?" Mitchell said.

"Not much Mitchell. Are you getting settled in okay?" Denise asked.

"Pretty much..."

"When is Andrea coming?"

"That's why I'm calling. She should be here in about two weeks." Mitchell responded.

"Good. Are you excited?"

"I am but I don't think she is," Mitchell said with doubt.

"Why would you say that?" Denise asked.

"She doesn't seem to be excited about it. I've been calling and she never says anything about it. Now I'm calling and she's not even answering the phone."

"Have you tried to call her at work?"

"Yes but all I get is an answering service." Mitchell said.

"Well you need to give her some time Mitchell."

"Give her time for what Denise?" Mitchell asked a little irritated.

"She has not healed. She seems to be harboring negative feelings about what happened between you and her sister."

"She's over that Denise, I'm back home."

Indiscretions of a Married Man

"I hate to be the one to tell you but that doesn't mean shit. She let you move in to mend the marriage but that doesn't mean it'll mend her heart. Her heart is broken Mitchell and when she drinks her pain comes to surface."

"I guess you're right but it seems as though our relationship is better than it was before." Mitchell said.

"Don't be fooled, your wife is wounded internally." Denise said.

"Damn I don't know what to do?"

"Well one thing you need to realize is that just because your wife let you come home doesn't mean that everything is okay." Denise said.

"Hate to say it but that is exactly what I was thinking."

"You may want to rethink a few things Mitchell." His cousin said.

"I hear you. Well thanks for the knowledge cousin."

"Talk to you later Mitchell," Denise said and hung up the phone.

Mitchell sat with the phone in his hand a few minutes as he replayed everything Denise said to him. He wondered why his wife had not called. They had not spoken to each other in over two weeks. She was supposed to be joining him in Charleston this Saturday and she was still working, he wondered why. He tried to control his imagination but his heart told him something wasn't right.

Indiscretions of a Married Man

Mitchell awoke early Saturday and called Andrea, still no answer. He immediately decided to get into his car and drive to Atlanta. He needed to see what was going on with his wife and why was she not answering his calls.

Mitchell pulled into his driveway, Andrea's truck wasn't there and the house looked rather deserted. He used his key to get in. As he slowly opened the door Mitchell was not prepared for what now faced him. The house was completely empty. There was not a picture hanging on the wall, not a curtain over a window. Everything was gone, it was no wonder that the phone continuously rang without answer there was nothing here that said someone lived here. He slowly walked through the house in disbelief. "What in the hell is going on?" Mitchell asked himself aloud as he crept up the stairs. Mitchell walked into what used to be their bedroom and stared at the empty room, he walked into the closet there was no trace of clothes, dazed he walked into the master bath and stared at the mirror, it was covered with big letters that read, "Goodbye Mitchell, Have a good life!" His entire body went numb as he stared at the words written across the mirror in red lipstick. The thought of Andrea just walking out of his life forever without warning brought tears to his eyes. Mitchell stood there and broke down, he cried for a very long time. He stood stationary for what seemed like an eternity before he exited down the steps to the front door. As he walked through the front door Mitchell attempted to wipe his face with his hand. "They say payback is a bitch," he said as he closed the door behind him. He drove off looking at the house through his rearview mirror until it disappeared. Mitchell began to rethink back to the last night they had spent together and he realized Andrea knew then she was leaving him. He had been so full of himself he hadn't heard what it was she was really saying. "It's time to move forward." Mitchell heard himself say aloud as he traveled back to Charleston alone.

Chapter 46

Andrea and Sharon had hung the last picture and unpacked the last box. "This is a lot of space Andrea. This townhouse is pretty big."

"I know but I have a lot of stuff."

"You didn't leave Mitchell much. What are you going to do with the house?" Sharon asked.

"I guess I will need to discuss that with Mitchell eventually," Andrea sighed.

Sharon stared at her for a moment wondering if her friend was sure about what she was doing. "You sure you're ready for this Andrea?"

"I am. Thanks for helping me get settled in. You know my dad was more than happy to move me once I told him I was going to be filing for divorce." They both smiled at the thought.

Indiscretions of a Married Man

"What changed your mind Andrea I thought you were trying to work it out?"

I thought so too but I was wrong. I just couldn't do it. I couldn't erase the vision of Mitchell and Monica together no matter how hard I tried." Andrea confessed.

"Not so easy is it?" Sharon asked.

"No girl it's not. You were right. I found myself having to get drunk to be with him. When we went to Charleston I got ripped and how I really felt came out to anyone who would listen."

"When did you decide to leave him?" Andrea asked.

"When we got back, he had this attitude because I embarrassed him. He had some nerve!"

"Damn sure did!" Andrea said.

"Sharon, he made some nasty comment about the way I acted in Charleston and I thought to myself who the hell is he, after what he's put me through! …And then he slept in the guest room for a week! I just felt that eventually we would be back where we were before all of this mess and I couldn't see myself there because I have changed and so has he."

"Why didn't you just tell him Andrea?" Sharon asked.

"I didn't want him to be able to change my mind and at that time I wasn't 100% sure. I still love him Sharon I just can't be with him after all that has happened. It's funny because I truly believed that I could." Andrea said.

"You just need a little time girl." Sharon assured her.

Indiscretions of a Married Man

"...Time for what?' Andrea almost busted out in laughter. "All the time in the world won't change the way I now feel. Besides we had time and it didn't work for me. The more he was around me the more I despised him. Then he began to get arrogant and I began to feel as though I wanted a little satisfaction of my own." Andrea said as she walked into the kitchen.

"Alright girl..." Sharon heard a pop from the kitchen. "What was that?"

Andrea walked back into the living room with a bottle of champagne in one hand and two glasses in the other. "It's celebration time!" Andrea said as she poured the champagne. Andrea then gave Sharon a hug and said, "Thanks for letting me find my own way."

"Not a problem at all. Here's to happiness." Sharon toasted.

"To happiness," Andrea repeated as they took their first sip of champagne. As she sipped she wondered was this truly the beginning of happiness for her......

Chapter 47

Mitchell sat in the middle of his living room floor gazing at its emptiness. He had not purchased furniture because he had been so sure his wife was going to join him along with their furniture.

Indiscretions of a Married Man

Since that had not happened he was now forced to rethink quite a few things.

Since returning from Atlanta he had spent several nights home alone wondering would he ever be able to forgive himself for the mess he had made of his life. It had become very lonely. For the past couple of weeks Mitchell had developed a routine of work and home. Tonight he decided to get out in an attempt to feel better. It had been three weeks since returning from Atlanta and it was now time to stop wallowing in self pity and take charge of his life.

Mitchell walked into his bedroom, showered and dressed. He wasn't sure where he was going tonight but was positive that it would be out of his apartment. Preparing to leave Mitchell took a final glance in the mirror to ensure he was presentable to the public. As he critiqued his reflection in the mirror, the phone rang. He tore himself away from the mirror to answer the phone wondering who could be calling on a Friday night.

"Hello," Mitchell answered.

"Hello. Mitchell?"

"This is he."

"Hey this is Tracy."

"Who…?" Mitchell asked.

"Tracy from Atlanta, remember Taboo?" she said a little disappointed.

"Oh yeah… Yeah. How are you?" Mitchell asked cautiously wondering how she'd gotten his phone number.

Indiscretions of a Married Man

"I'm fine. What about yourself?" Tracy detected an edge in Mitchell's voice.

"I can't complain. It's been quite a while since we've last talked."

"It's only been three weeks, if that Mitchell." Tracy said as she begins to think this may not have been a good idea.

"Three weeks?" Mitchell was no longer able to conceal his confusion.

"Oh so you don't remember calling me about three weeks ago? It was about two o'clock in the morning and you were pretty toasted. You don't remember? We talked for an hour. I could see how you can't remember." Tracy tried to jog his memory.

The line went silent as Mitchell thought very hard to remember and the memory of the night in question slowly began to evolve. He'd gotten a little more than toasted. It had been a week after he'd returned from Atlanta. He made a stop at the liquor store after work and bought a fifth of Crown Black. Once he got home he tuned in on some jazz, one of his favorites, *'The Best of Najee.'* He began to sip on his drink, the next thing he knew it was Saturday morning and he definitely didn't remember any call.

"Are you still there Mitchell?" Tracy asked.

"Yes I am. So what's up?" Mitchell asked.

"I'm in town and thought we could spend some time together."

"Lady your timing is so perfect! I was just about to step out of the door." Mitchell began to feel better about the night. Things were looking up and it had not gotten started yet.

"Well where were you going?" Tracy asked.

"I'm not really sure. Just out! Do you have any suggestions?" Mitchell asked.

"I know a few spots. Do you feel like any company?"

"I wouldn't mind at all." Mitchell felt quite relieved at the thought of not having to go out alone. Tracy gave Mitchell directions to the hotel she was staying in for the weekend. He picked Tracy up and they began their evening with a bite to eat in downtown Charleston. Afterwards they partied until four in the morning. Mitchell was feeling pretty nice and did not want to go home alone. It had been three weeks and he was more than ready.

Mitchell turned towards Tracy and asked, "Would you like to bring the morning in together?"
Tracy leaned over and lightly kissed Mitchell's lips, "I would love that." Mitchell began to drive towards his home.

Chapter 48

It had been one month since Andrea had left Mitchell and as much as she tried to shake his memory she could not. Andrea had begun to go out and drink more than she normally did when she was

Indiscretions of a Married Man

with Mitchell. She had just gotten out of class, it was Friday and she was meeting Sharon at the Mexican restaurant on Old National Hwy in College Park. Andrea had forgotten how nice it was to be getting off of work in the afternoon. As Andrea pulled into the parking lot she noticed Sharon's car. Sharon was seated at the bar and she had already ordered their first round of tequila shots accompanied by a medium pitcher of Modelo beer. "Just what I need after a rough week," Andrea said as she reached her stool.

Andrea and Sharon sat comfortably at the bar and talked over three more rounds of tequila. Feeling pretty good they decided to play a game of pool. After losing the game Andrea decided to end the evening and pay their bill while Sharon went to the ladies room. Andrea approached the bar and noticed two gentleman seated. "You're not leaving are you?" the younger of the two spoke.
Eye candy was Andrea's first thought, "I certainly am..." She responded.

"Can I buy you another drink before you leave?" He responded.

"That depends on my friend." Andrea knew she was already feeling tipsy but he was too cute to say no.

"I'll buy her one too. Where is she?" He insisted.

"She's coming up right behind you." Andrea said as Sharon approached them.

"Sharon this gentleman would like to buy us a drink before we leave."

Indiscretions of a Married Man

"I think I'll pass Andrea. I'm feeling pretty good already."Sharon said.

"What about you? Would you like a drink?" The younger guy faced Andrea directing his question to her.

"Sure…" Andrea replied.

"That's 1 shot of tequila coming up…" He said as they introduced themselves to each other. His name was Jesse.

As Andrea waited for her drink, Sharon eyed her to let her know she was ready to go and although Andrea noticed, she continued to chat with Jesse. They exchanged quite a bit of information about each other over their drink while Sharon sat irritated. Their conversation seemed to be going well and Jesse discreetly invited Andrea to come home with him. Not expecting her to say yes because he had only known her for one hour. Who could be so lucky? They chatted until she finished her tequila and then all three exited the café. Sharon left in her car driving towards her home. Andrea got into her car but instead of driving towards her home she followed Jesse towards his.

The sun beamed brightly through the window awakening Andrea. As she rolled over she realized she was in a strange bed with someone on the other side. Slowly her memory began to fade in and she remembered she had followed Jesse to his house and once they entered his house they stripped down to nakedness and ate each other up like it was their last meal.

Indiscretions of a Married Man

As Andrea remembered she became angry with herself. She eased out of the bed and quietly began to get dressed. Not wanting to wake him and spare her the embarrassment. Once dressed, she grabbed her purse and shoes, tiptoed down the steps and out of the front door. Andrea was sure she had escaped an embarrassing moment by tipping out while he slept. Not realizing if she had looked his way just once she would have seen he was awake from the moment she eased out of his bed. He wanted to erase the memory of her being there as well.

Chapter 49

It had been ten days since Mitchell had received the call from Tracy on that Friday night and she was still here. Friday night after their date Tracy went home with Mitchell. Saturday morning Mitchell suggested her spending the rest of the weekend with him rather than give the hotel more money. They went shopping and she helped Mitchell select furniture for his home. It had been a lot of fun and the weekend had turned out to be quite enjoyable. But by Sunday Mitchell was ready for her to leave. He missed his personal space and wanted to reclaim it. Sunday came and went without Tracy making any effort to leave. She seemed quite comfortable and acted as though this was a permanent arrangement. After a couple of

Indiscretions of a Married Man

days passed and Tracy gave no indication that she planned on leaving, Mitchell began inquiring about her commitments in Atlanta. The responses she gave ensured him she was contemplating permanent residency with him. Mitchell became very uncomfortable with the entire situation and he wasn't sure how to fix it.

Mitchell sat at his desk as he had done for the past seven days wondering how he was going to get her out of his home. "Damn all I wanted was a little weekend ass not a permanent roommate!" Mitchell said angrily as he placed his head in his hands. Totally frustrated he thought long and hard on how to get her out without actually telling her to get out. He didn't have a hard enough heart to do that. Another two days of pondering passed before Mitchell had finally figured it out.

Friday after a full day of work Mitchell felt better than he had in two weeks. He had persuaded Tracy to ride to Atlanta with him to complete some unfinished business. She packed very few items because she had every intention of returning but Mitchell had a different plan.

Once they arrived into Atlanta, Mitchell checked them into the Holiday Inn for two nights. He then sent Tracy up to the room with her overnight bag alone under the pretense that he needed to handle his business before he joined her. Mitchell then drove away from the hotel without looking back. After driving 10 minutes away from the hotel Mitchell began to doubt what he had just done, definitely not feeling good about what he had just did. His first instinct was to call Darien; he hesitated for a brief moment before deciding. "What the hell?" Mitchell said as he picked up the phone realizing it was time to mend and heal. "Hello…Darien?"

"Yes? Is this Mitchell?" Darien asked in complete surprise.

"Hey. I was wondering if I could come by…"

"You know you are my brother no matter what you're always welcome." Darien said.

Mitchell was surprised as well as grateful that his college friend was so welcoming after the last conversation they had and how abruptly he had left. He realized an apology was in order. Mitchell was knocking at Darien's door an hour later with a fifth of Crown Royal in his hand as a peace offering. Darien opened his door to Mitchell and gave him a sincere and warm embrace. They talked late into the night about their college days and what it was that had brought Darien into his homosexuality. He then told Darien that it was Tracy who initially brought him to Atlanta this weekend. They laughed about it and as usual Darien put the situation with Tracy into perspective for him and afterwards Mitchell didn't feel bad at all.

Saturday afternoon Mitchell was on the road back to Charleston. After getting in and taking a hot shower Mitchell began checking his messages. Tracy had blown his phone up, she had left eight messages and they all said the same thing in different words, that Mitchell wasn't shit for leaving her at the hotel in Atlanta. She also gave him her mother's address to forward her remaining

Indiscretions of a Married Man

belonging. Once Mitchell erased all eight messages he turned out the light, happy to be in his bed alone and said to out loud, "Time to change the phone number."

Chapter 50

Andrea decided that it would be best if she slowed down on going out after the incident at the Mexican restaurant. She had never done anything like that before and was sure that the tequila had given her the nerve to do it. When the tequila had worn off the next morning the picture was very disturbing and ugly. She had not spoken to Sharon since that night because she knew she would ask questions and that was a night she wanted to forget. She could not believe how she had played herself. Jesse never even bothered to call her afterwards, "What a bastard!" she thought.

For the past couple of weeks Andrea went to work and returned home. She began bringing work home with her to stay focused. She had converted her sunroom into her office and everything she needed to perform her job at home was there. It was Saturday afternoon and she sat at her computer with stacks of work at her feet. She had been at her computer for over three hours and was becoming distracted as well as restless. Andrea gazed out of the window enjoying the view she had of the pool. She finally decided a

Indiscretions of a Married Man

break was in order and decided to take a swim and soak up the sun's rays. Andrea put on her bikini and slipped a skirt over her bikini bottoms so that she wouldn't appear naked as she walked to the pool. She then prepared herself a small pitcher of rum and coke grabbed a towel and strolled to the pool.

She was the only person at the pool and looked forward to the solitude. It was like being in a private pool. She eased into the warm water and began to swim laps. She completed five laps before she grew tired of the water. Not yet ready to go back home and slave to the computer, she decided to sit and enjoy the sun while she enjoyed her cocktail. As she dried off the property maintenance man approached her casually. "Enjoying the water?" He asked.

"Yes I am." Andrea smiled.

"I'm Terry the maintenance man."

"I know who you are. I have seen you around on the property."

"Do you mind if I sit?"Terry asked.

"No not at all." Andrea answered as she continued to sip her drink.

They sat by the pool talking about nothing of importance but quite entertaining. It began to get dark and Andrea had finished her pitcher of rum and coke, which was nice and strong and had her feeling nice as well. She rose from her seat and Terry invited her to his apartment for anther drink, because she was more restless now than before and did not want to resort back to her lonely townhome she accepted his offer. He looked harmless enough, Andrea thought as she followed him to his apartment.

Once inside Andrea took a seat, it wasn't long after she sat that she questioned herself as to why she was even there. "I have to stop drinking, it make me make poor decision." She thought to herself. The studio home he lived in had one sofa and a small stereo that sat on the floor. There was a small television but there were no pictures, plants, or anything else that one would acquire after being in a place for a while, especially as the maintenance man. Andrea began to have very strong doubts, feeling uncomfortable she decided to leave. Just as she stood to leave Terry came out of the kitchen with two Budweiser beers. "You weren't about to leave were you?" Terry asked.

"Yeah I was." Andrea said moving towards the door.

"Why?" Terry asked.

"I just got a little tired." Andrea did not want to tell him the truth because it would hurt his feelings and she didn't want to look stupid for being here in the first place. But as she spoke she felt stupid so she sat back down. He sat across from her and lit a marijuana cigarette. "Do you smoke?" He asked.

"Yes but not that often." Andrea said.

"Would you like to smoke?" He asked as he passed her the marijuana cigarette.

"Not really, I don't smoke like that," Andrea said.

Indiscretions of a Married Man

"Oh come on, one pull is not going to kill you…" He assured her.

"Why not…?" Andrea thought as she reached for the cigarette. She inhaled deeply several times before Terry got up and locked the door; he also turned the music up very loud. She passed him the marijuana cigarette and he declined. Andrea put the cigarette out because not only was she high but their conversation began to make her a little uncomfortable. He began to elaborate on how he felt woman put themselves in dangerous situation and they were deserving of whatever they got. From his conversation Andrea got the impression that he had a problem with women. He got up to get them another beer and returned to sit but this time he sat next to her with a glazed look in his eyes. "I think I'd better be going." Andrea said out of fear.

"Oh come on drink your beer first." He said handing her an open beer. Andrea took the beer and tried to drink it as quickly as she could so that she could leave. She felt very uncomfortable as they sat in silence listening to the music he had turned up quite loud. "Do you know that if I wanted to I could rape you or even murder you and no one would ever know because no one knows where you are right now?" It seemed as though his voice had changed to monotone. The change in his voice startled Andrea more than what he was saying had.

"Excuse me?" Andrea asked becoming very nervous.

Indiscretions of a Married Man

"I said no one knows where you are right now and I could basically do whatever I'd like to you... Another stupid bitch...!"

"I think I'd better leave." Andrea said nervously as she stood up in an attempt to leave. But as she stood he stood as well. He harshly pushed her back down on the sofa. "What's your rush?" He asked as he stood directly in front of her.

"I need to leave, please move out of my way." Andrea stood and was face to face with him. She attempted once again to move towards the door. But Terry grabbed her and wrestled her back on the sofa. He grabbed her face and forced his tongue into her mouth. His sweaty hands were all over her; he was much stronger than he looked. He grabbed at her skirt and bikini bottoms yanking them down past her knees. He viciously groped at her crotch... he actually grabbed it and shoved his finger inside of her. After he fingered her for several moments as she wrestled him, he released her and stood up. He watched her intensely as she nervously pulled up her clothes. After Andrea pulled her clothes up she was so nervous and upset her hands trembled preventing her from getting the door unlocked and getting out of there. Terry stepped to the door unlocked and opened it with a smirk on his face. As Andrea ran through the door she heard Terry say, "Be more careful next time baby."

Andrea didn't stop running until she was behind the locked door of her home crying hysterically. She felt humiliated and alone. She wanted someone to protect her. She missed having the security blanket of having a husband, someone to protect her from the craziness of trying to date. Andrea followed her first instinct and through blurred vision she dialed Mitchell's home phone number. *"The number you have reached has been disconnected. Please check the number and dial again."* Andrea hung up the phone and dialed again making sure she had dialed the correct number. She heard the same message. Andrea stared at the phone as if trying to will the number connected. "I guess he has completely accepted us being over and I need to accept it as well. I guess it is time to file for divorce.

Chapter 51

"Mitchell, how are you? We haven't heard from you in a while." Darien asked.

"I've just been taking it easy." Mitchell said, surprised to hear from his friend.

"Have you been out exploring Charleston yet?" Darien asked.

"No the last time I went out I didn't have such a great experience and then after Tracy tried to move in on me I decided to relax from the date scene for a while." Mitchell said.

Indiscretions of a Married Man

"Hell if you have a computer you don't have to leave the house to date. Do you have Internet?" Darien asked.

"Yes as of yesterday." Mitchell said, glad he decided to purchase a laptop so that he could do work at home.

"Have you heard of Plenty of Fish?" Darien asked

"No, what is it?" Mitchell asked.

"It's a site that allows you to hook up with people across the country. You get to pick and choose. Try it, I guarantee you'll like it." Darien said,

"This is not a gay site is it? You know I don't get down like that!" Mitchell asked.

"Hell no man…!" Darien laughed.

"Ok then, maybe I'll do that tonight." Mitchell said.

"Well let me know how it works out."

"Will keep you posted." Mitchell said.

"I'll talk with you later." Darien said.

"Thanks for calling man. Take care." Mitchell hung up the phone and quickly wrote on paper "Plenty of Fish" so that he would not forget because he was definitely going to use it.

It had been almost four weeks since Darien had suggested Plenty of Fish to Mitchell and he had been on it every chance he got. Mitchell registered himself as Mr. Tall, Dark and Successful and completed a profile. Although many of those registered, had photos of themselves on their web page, Mitchell thought that was too much for him, he was not comfortable with knowing anyone going to his

Indiscretions of a Married Man

web page would see his face, therefore he chose not to post his picture on his site. Each day he would get in from work, check his mail on POF, and there was always mail for him. He had initiated a few contacts himself and he talked to quite a few ladies across the country, Sunshine in Florida, Ladybug in Texas, Sable in California and Chocolate in Atlanta. Some of them had pictures and others did not. Those without pictures he was a bit leery about and chose not to spend a lot of time chatting back and forth with them. As vain as that seemed he just did not want any surprises.

There was one exception, and that exception was Chocolate from Atlanta. He chatted with her quite often and she had no picture of herself posted. According to their chats she was single, had no children, and from the description she had given of herself, she was very attractive. Although she didn't have a picture and he had no idea what she looked like, he truly enjoyed her conversation. She came on at 11:45 almost every night and they would talk. She seemed so familiar and it seemed as though they had so much in common. Darien was definitely right, this was so much better than going to the club standing around waiting to be chosen.

He found himself looking forward to getting home 11:45 so that they could talk and the more they talked the more Mitchell wondered what she really looked like. He was beginning to like her quite a bit and it would soon be time for them to meet. He was very excited about that.

Indiscretions of a Married Man

After a year of trying to come to terms with his separation from Andrea he could finally say he was all right. It had been a long road and a few months ago Mitchell could not see past Andrea but thanks to his computer and POF it seemed as though he would finally be able to move on and feel good about it.

Chapter 52

The day after Andrea's near rape she went to the Management office to inquire on the maintenance man named Terry and to her surprise they had no one employed at that property by that name. The apartment number she gave them according to their records was scheduled for eviction within seven days and should have been vacant. Once again she had exercised bad judgment because of alcohol and this time she could have gotten seriously hurt. It could have been a lot worse. This information shook Andrea so bad she went into seclusion.

Earlier in the year Andrea's job had offered quite a few people in her department the flexibility of working from her home, at that time she had declined but after the last incident she had, she went to Human Resources to inquire on whether it was still being offered and to her surprise it was. Within two weeks Andrea was working from home and she loved it. She barely left the house, her work and play was done right from her home office. With her computer and the services Internet offered she had no need to go anywhere.

Chapter 53

As Mitchell put the key in the lock he heard his phone ringing on the other side of the door. He ran through the door in an attempt to answer the phone before the answering service picked up. He did manage to intercept the answering service and answer the call. "Darien! What's going on?"

"Hey Mitchell, I've got a couple of tickets to the Falcons game and thought you'd like get away for a weekend." Darien said.

"When is the game?"

"Two weeks from today."

"I'll be there." Mitchell said.

"One of the guys that went with us to the races gets free tickets and a couple of the guys decided to make a day of it. So can we count you in?"

"You know that! Thanks for the invite." Mitchell said.

"Anytime… Call if anything changes, otherwise I look forward to seeing you in two weeks."

Indiscretions of a Married Man

"I'll do that." Mitchell and Darien said their goodbyes and hung up the phone.

Mitchell went from the phone and directly to the Internet. Once on, he logged into POF and began to check his mail. As he checked his mail an instant pager popped up, it was Chocolate in Atlanta. A smile stretched across Mitchell's face as he began to read. *"Hey Mr. TDS... How's your day going?"*

"It is going good since I've taken a vacation day and don't have to go in to work tonight. What about yours?" Mitchell typed as fast as he could anxious to read her every reply.

"Well my day is not quite over. I'm putting in a little overtime." Chocolate answered.

"I am surprised that you are on this early in the day normally I can't get you until the night." Mitchell said.

"Well my schedule has changed and I have flexed hours now!" Chocolate answered.

"That must be quite nice." Mitchell said.

"Yeah it is."

"So everything otherwise is going okay for you?" Mitchell was trying to ease into asking her out once he got to Atlanta.

"You won't get any complaints from me."

"I just received a call from a friend of mine inviting me to Atlanta in two weeks."

"What's the occasion?" She typed in.

"He's got opening tickets to the Falcons game."

Indiscretions of a Married Man

"That sounds like fun."

"Are you into sports?" Mitchell asked

"No I can't say that I am." Chocolate answered.

"Well I thought that maybe we could get together and perhaps have dinner while I am there." Mitchell suggested.

"Smile..." She typed in to let him know she was smiling.

"Well I'm glad you're smiling, but would that be a yes or is that a yes?"

"Have to go, will talk with you later."

"What about my answer?" Mitchell insisted.

"Bye!" Chocolate logged out.

Mitchell sat back and stared at the monitor knowing she had signed off. He smiled with the comfort of knowing that she had not said no which meant she was as interested in him as he was in her. There was life after Andrea after all...

<u>Epilogue</u>

Mitchell had selected a seat at the bar with a perfect view of the front entrance. Chocolate had finally agreed to going out with Mitchell once he got to Atlanta. They had agreed upon a secluded and small dinner bar in Cobb County. He didn't want to be distracted by anything or anyone. This was to be a special evening and he hoped that she would not be disappointed. He believed that he could not be disappointed at this point regardless of what she looked like because he had developed an attraction for her just from the conversations they'd shared.

After asking Chocolate to dinner he had not heard from her for a week. He thought he had frightened her off and had begun to lose that good feeling. Three days before it was time for Mitchell to leave for Atlanta, he decided to check his email on POF. There were plenty of messages, but there was only one he was concerned with and that was the one from Chocolate. It simply read, "Yes I will have dinner with you." Mitchell immediately emailed her back and they made plans to meet at 7:00 p.m. on Saturday. Mitchell had given Chocolate a detailed description of the black suit he would be wearing as she had given him a detailed description of the brown dress she would be wearing and now Mitchell was here waiting for her to walk through the door.

He had drunk a double shot of cognac and chased it with a beer in the attempt to calm his nerves as he waited. Instead of calming his nerves he suddenly had to use the men's room. As he walked out of the men's room and towards the bar his heart skipped a beat. There was a woman wearing the brown dress he had been given such a detailed description of at the bar. Her back was turned to him but from what he could see she was everything she described herself to be. Mitchell tried to calm himself as he walked up to her. He lightly tapped her on her shoulder, "Chocolate?"

Indiscretions of a Married Man

As she slowly turned Mitchell's mouth dropped as wide open as it possibly could. "Andrea?"

"Mitchell?"

"You're Chocolate?" Mitchell asked a bit confused.

"Yes and I am going to assume that you are Mr. TDS." Andrea asked quite amused.

"Yes I am." As they stood facing each other in total disbelief, a smile slowly extended itself across Mitchell's face. This shit cannot be happening! Mitchell said as he paid her a compliment. "You look very good tonight Chocolate." He said with many thoughts going through his head.

"And so do you." Andrea said with a smile of her own. She also thought to herself, "This shit cannot be happening! What now!"